Praise for *Vamped*

"Move over, Buffy! Lucienne Diver transfuses some fresh blood into the vampire genre. Feisty, fashionable, and fun—*Vamped* is a story readers will sink their teeth into and finish thirsty for more."

—*Mari Mancusi, author of*
The Blood Coven Vampires *series*

"This book rollicks along, full of humor, romance, and action. Gina is a smart-aleck heroine worth reading about, a sort of teenage Betsy Taylor (*Undead and Unwed*) with a lot of Cher Horowitz (*Clueless*) thrown in. Fans of Katie Maxwell will devour *Vamped*."

—*Rosemary Clement-Moore, author of*
Prom Dates from Hell

"I really sank my teeth into Lucienne Diver's *Vamped*. A fun, frothy teenage romp with lots of action, a little shopping, and a cute vampire guy. Who could ask for more?"

—*Marley Gibson, author of*
Ghost Huntress: The Awakening

This one's for Ty, who makes my life so much sweeter.

LUCIENNE DIVER

Vamped

flux™
Woodbury, Minnesota

First Edition
First Printing, 2009

Book design by Steffani Sawyer
Cover design by Lisa Novak
Cover image © 2009 Corbis/Jupiterimages Corporation

Flux, an imprint of Llewellyn Publications

Library of Congress Cataloging-in-Publication Data
Diver, Lucienne, 1971–
  Vamped / Lucienne Diver.—1st ed.
      p. cm.
  Summary: After being turned into a vampire, Gina realizes that she, along with many other students from her high school, have become pawns for an uprising within the vampire-world.
  ISBN 978-0-7387-1474-5
  [1. Vampires—Fiction. 2. Revolutions—Fiction. 3. High schools—Fiction. 4. Schools—Fiction. 5. Friendship—Fiction. 6. Dating (Social customs)—Fiction.] I. Title.
  PZ7.D6314Vam 2009
  [Fic]—dc22

                                        2008053351

Flux
Llewellyn Publications
A Division of Llewellyn Worldwide, Ltd.
2143 Wooddale Drive, Dept. 978-0-7387-1474-5
Woodbury, MN 55125-2989, U.S.A.
www.fluxnow.com

Printed in the United States of America

———

Excerpt from "Valley Vamp Rules for Surviving Your Senior Prom" by Gina Covello, spring issue of *Modern Goth Magazine*.

1. Don't go strapless. I don't care how sexy you think it is, you're going to spend half the night tugging your dress back into place. If by some miracle it's tight enough to stay put, chances are you've got overhang. And let me just say for the record, "Ew."

2. Do *not* get so loaded at the after-prom party that you accidentally-on-purpose end up in the broom closet with the surprise hottie of the evening— say, the class chess champ who's somewhere lost his Coke-bottle lenses and undergone an extreme makeover—especially if that makeover has anything to do with becoming one of the undead.

3. If because of said chess champ's ridiculously irresistible vamp mojo you're compelled to skip Rule #2, do not let your extremely jealous boyfriend—let's call him "Chaz"—catch you.

4. Never get into a car, no matter how well the cherry red finish goes with your gown, with anyone who's been drinking or just found you in a compromising position with the mother of all hickeys forming on your neck—just for example.

5. If you've ignored the previous rules—and I mean, seriously, give some thought to #1 (talk about wardrobe malfunction)—make sure you have a death plan. It's kinda like an emergency plan, but, you know, for death. For example, make sure there's absolutely nothing in your closet you wouldn't be caught dead in, because it's a freakin' guarantee that's what they'll dress you in for the viewing. You may also want to leave some kind of instructions behind about not being buried for four days—at which point you're either risen or beyond caring—because digging yourself out of the ground, not to mention prying open the damned coffin, is hell on your manicure.

6. Now, chances are that in the midst of everything, Rule #5 never even popped up on your radar. I get that. So, you're famished and filthy, but hey, you've survived—better than a certain somebody's cherry red convertible, anyway. Now, to keep up this trend. Normally, I don't advocate going out in public without freshening up, so here's a tip: blood is never fashion-forward. Chances are that as a newly risen vamp, you're going to be a bit, um, indelicate in your feeding, so you may want to eat first, shop later.

7. Here's where it gets dicey. Vamps have no reflection. Yeah, don't even get me started. No way at all to fix your hair and makeup. Who wants to go through eternity a total shlub? I mean, what a cosmic joke, right? My recommendation: turn your own stylist, start an entourage—whatever it takes.

8. Okay, so you're fed, you're fab. Chances are your geek-boy sire is waiting in the wings somewhere expecting you to be his sex slave for all eternity. Girls, all I can say is I don't care if the man is the second coming of Brad Pitt, you make him work for it. Begin as you mean to continue. You're young, beautiful, and, as long as you avoid stakes and beheadings, immortal. The world is your oyster. Make him crack it open and set the pearls (preferably in platinum).

1

I'm here to tell you, rising from the dead just purely sucks. I woke in a blind terror. Literally blind ... my eyelids tried to flip upward like cartoon window shades as consciousness kicked my butt, but they got nowhere fast. Something was holding my lids shut. My hands banged against the sides of my prison as I tried to raise them to my eyes, and a scream bubbled up from somewhere around my toes, but nothing came out of my mouth. *Oh God*, my mind gibbered—*no breath!* No air. I was suffocating.

A microsecond later I realized how silly that was. I couldn't suffocate because I wasn't breathing. No heartbeat either. In fact, all was silent as ... well, as the grave.

My mind stuttered to a halt. Somehow, I didn't think that was just, you know, a simile or metaphor or ... whatever. No heartbeat equaled no pulse. No pulse equaled dead, right? And yet here I was. I fought down my rising panic—no, too calm a word—*hysteria*, with great unnecessary breaths ... until my inner *Cosmo* girl witch-slapped me with an order to put on my big girl panties and deal with it. I was Gina Covello, dammit. I'd survive now, panic later.

Okay, there was only one way I knew to wake up dead— well, two, but I didn't feel like a flesh-eating zombie. So I must be, like, a vampire. A creature of the night, as in Bram Stoker, Anne Rice, and all that jazz. That could be cool, right? I mean, beyond the sucking blood and pointy-stick phobia, there was eternal youth and beauty and all ... assuming I found a way out of the grave. Otherwise, it wouldn't much matter. I'd be doomed to unlife, watching the worms crawl in and the worms crawl out, *the worms play pinochle on your snout* ... the childhood rhyme played in my head.

Ack! I felt around, appreciating that my parents must have sprung for the deluxe model coffin with silk lining and all, and managed with some squiggling to get my fingers up to my eyelids, which—ewwww—were held shut by creepy plastic things that felt like tiny, spiny sea urchins.

Gross! I didn't remember Buffy-verse vamps having these kinds of problems.

I tossed the freakshow eyelid doohickeys aside and moved straight into screaming for help (after filling my lungs like balloons so that I had air to force through my vocal cords) and pounding on the lid of my coffin. Ten or twenty blows later, things were actually popping and I figured this whole unlife thing must have imparted some cool superhuman strength to me. Either that or my grave hadn't had enough visitors yet to really pack down the earth, which stood to reason. I'd only been dead three days, if the legends could be trusted. My parents, if they ran true to form, had probably taken themselves off to some exotic locale right after the funeral to drink away the discomfort of my death. It wouldn't be so much that they didn't care as that they didn't *like* caring. Emotion messed with their Botox treatments, causing unsightly wrinkles and all. Crying made you blotchy.

Superhuman strength or no, by the time I broke through to the surface, my manicure was totally shot, my nails were split, and I was covered in dirt. And I mean covered. I was about to wig out when I realized just what I was brushing off—and one shock kind of cancelled out the other. My parents had buried me in a truly heinous dress of white eyelet, which made me look like a stylistically challenged child bride. I had a vague repressed memory of being forced to wear it to my first communion years ago and marveled that it still fit. Not that I'd grown out, except for, you know, up top. Sadly, I hadn't done much growing *up* either; I'd maxed out at, like, five foot nothing. Anyway, if anything deserved to be covered in grave dust, it was this old rag.

I shook out my mane of black hair, trying not to think of all the things that might have fallen into it. Had there been maggots? *Oh please, please, please don't let there have been maggots.* I forced that mental image down into a deep dark mental box labeled *Spiders and all things icky*, but somehow lifting the lid unleashed a hoard of other creepy crawly thoughts. The memory swarm knocked me to my butt on the fresh earth of my grave.

I had a pretty good idea of how I'd become a vamp. I had flashes of prom gowns, yelling, screaming, Chaz hauling me around by the arm, his breath smelling of cheap beer, tossing me into his car, swerving all over the road, the painful shriek of metal on metal as we were sideswiped by a green muscle car, spinning out, a tree rushing at me *way too fast* ...

I brought my mental shield crashing down on the memory that followed: the world careening out of control, the sudden shock of impact, and ... Anyway, that was how I died, not how I'd become a vamp—which must have happened earlier, I thought, at the post-prom party when I'd somehow found myself necking with Bobby-freakin'-Delvecchio, who'd become all mysteriously irresistible. And yeah, there'd been a bit of nipping involved too, which must have been where the whole blood-exchange thing took place. The details were a little fuzzy, maybe due to having dipped into Marcy's punch, but that was probably just as well.

My stomach gave a lurch. I thought at first it was a rebellious reaction against the idea of blood, but then recognized it as hunger—no, *bloodlust*. I cringed. Well, that sealed it. Despite my attempt to sunny it up, undead equaled uncool. I was starting to realize why vamp films qualified as horror.

I mean, an all-liquid diet, a life without tanning options. I'd be doomed to an eternity looking like the bride of Frankenstein, especially in the gunnysack I was currently wearing. As soon as I got my hands on my sire, I was going to wring his scrawny little neck.

Speaking of which, you'd think the advantage to being turned by a geekboy like Bobby Delvecchio would be endless devotion, like he should be waiting for me to rise with a cup of warm blood and a spa robe or something. I flashed back to those Elijah Wood blue eyes of his and the way he'd looked prom night, with his kinda shaggy brown hair contrasting with his tailored tux. Okay, maybe not so geeky after all. Maybe his new vamp mojo had given him a totally inflated sense of himself as a ladies' man. He could be out flashing those baby blues at some other girl right now. Creating his own harem, even. The very thought made me rise again from the fresh earth of my grave, fists clenched.

"Gina!" As if I'd conjured him, Bobby's voice called out to me from across the cemetery. I almost turned toward him in relief before remembering I was mad at the two-timing bastard.

"Gina!" he yelled louder. "Wait."

I allowed him to approach me, timing my turn for when he was about three steps away—optimum range for the whirl-and-glare maneuver. I was kind of amazed at how well I was able to pinpoint his position; my new vamp senses made the tiniest sound seem full volume.

"You're late," I informed him, ignoring the fact that I'd nearly whapped him with my hair as I spun. I punctuated my comment with a hand to one hip.

Bobby looked like he wanted to pull on the collar of his shirt, only he wasn't really wearing one—a collar, that is. He had on a V-necked sweater the exact same shade as his eyes, and a black leather jacket that looked like it would be soft as butter. I wondered if the vamp transformation had given him supernatural fashion sense and, if so, why everyone wasn't doing it. It stopped the breath that I … wasn't using anyway. And that was beyond weird.

"Um, yeah," he answered, his ability to talk to girls still lagging behind his spankin' new style. "There was something I needed to do first."

That was when my eyes lit on the shopping bags. Two of them. That most gorgeous Macy's red. All my negativity just disappeared.

2

"Are those for me?" I asked.

When he nodded, I pounced and grabbed the bags. Bobby, startled, was wise enough to back away slowly. I had to drop one bag to paw through the other, which was bursting with the most gorgeous riot of fabrics—silks, satins, and fabrics not found in nature, all dyed in vivid gemstone hues. My heart nearly burst. I dropped the bag to pick up the second, heavier one—and found a jumble of strappy sandals, stylish boots, and a jewelry box that was long and narrow, just the right shape to hold a diamond tennis bracelet.

"I wasn't sure of your size," Bobby said, jutting his chin at the shoes, "so I got a bunch." He might have said something after that, but I couldn't hear him over the call of the blood-red Macy's bags, which was nearly as powerful as the bloodlust still tearing at me. Actually, the urge to shop and the urge to launch into a feeding frenzy were both pretty primal. Maybe Macy's had tapped into something there, like a vein.

I could have hugged Bobby for thinking of retail therapy—most men wouldn't—but I had a jewelry box to explore. Holding it in one palm, I lifted the lid. Drawing a breath, I let it out again in a sigh. A garnet choker lay nestled in the velvet, along with a set of matching earrings. Not diamonds, but they would do.

I moved to hug the boy, to show that all was forgiven, but was stopped in my tracks by a bright light aimed at my face.

"You there!" someone called from the direction of the light. The voice had that air of officialdom that said maybe there was a badge to back it up and we were in big, big trouble. "The cemetery's closed. What are you up to?"

We were spared for about a second as the light bobbed down to the bags at my feet and back up to our faces.

"Don't move. I'm gonna need to see what you've got in the bags, and I want some ID."

"Um, I've got receipts for those," Bobby said.

The light centered on him, and he averted his eyes. Based on the crunching of dirt and twigs, the rent-a-cop was coming closer. I was still all but blind. I wasn't sure what I should do anyway, but I had a bad feeling about this. All he'd have to do is recognize me, like from an obit or some news coverage of the accident (such a teen tragedy *had* to have been all over the news), but it was Bobby he focused on.

"You, boy, what's your name?"

"Bobby, uh, Beall."

The footsteps stopped just out of easy reach. "Uh-huh. And what're you doing in the cemetery after dark, Bobby, uh, Beall?"

"Meeting my girl."

"Uh-huh," the security guard repeated, shifting the light my way.

"You—you look like you've been digging in the dirt." His voice suddenly took on a much harder edge than it had before, like he was no longer just rousting us kids. I looked at Bobby, but he met my gaze with eyes wide and clueless. Meanwhile, the guard was glaring like he might taser me now and ask questions later.

"I'm just dirty from rolling around. You know, making out," I answered, brushing myself off self-consciously. "Ruined my best dress," it nearly killed me to add.

The polyester patrolman sneered at that. "We could go on all night with you lying to me and me not buying it, or you could just tell me what you're doing with the bodies."

I flinched back as if he'd slapped me. *Bodies?* As if.

I kicked over the closest bag and shoes went sprawling. "Footwear, okay? Happy birthday to me. No body parts. Ick!"

Something shifted in the guy's look, like my reaction was too totally true not to be believed, but still... cemetery. At night. Me looking like the walking dead. Not exactly the picture of innocence.

"I still need to see those IDs," he insisted. "Take 'em out, then put your hands up where I can see them."

Bobby's ID wouldn't say "Beall" and, of course, I had none at all. I didn't know what Bobby was doing when he reached into his jacket—stalling for time, maybe, but I didn't see any way of this ending well. So I did the only thing I could think of. I sacrificed my new pretties to fling the jewelry box straight at the light. It probably wouldn't have worked if I'd been the old Gina, but with my new vamp powers, even that little projectile had the force and speed to knock the light out of the guard's hands and send it spinning crazily into the night. *Cool!* I thought.

"Hey!" he cried.

I grabbed Bobby, grabbed the unspilled bag of clothes, and pulled them both in the direction of *away*, running hell-bent for leather. No bullets came zinging after us, though the pounding feet behind us indicated pursuit. We lost it after just a few blocks and three or four crazy zig-zags, and stopped in an alleyway between a deli and a thrift store to listen for absolute proof of our escape.

I felt like laughing maniacally. This whole vamp thing—it was crazy, but now that I'd had a taste, I felt drunk on power, jazzed with the rush of the ultimate high, more alive than I'd ever felt when I'd had a pulse.

I threw myself into Bobby's arms and nuzzled his neck. His scent was overwhelming. I could smell the blood beneath his skin, practically feel its call. It was like... like...*sexy*, intoxicating, kinda like the punch at the after-prom party. My eye teeth tingled and grew.

"I'm glad you came," I told him, half slicing my lip in the process. It stung, but only for a second. The hunger was stronger, and I licked away my own blood, totally in denial even as it happened.

"Well, sure," Bobby said. "When I heard about the accident... You are my girl, right?"

I'd completely lost track of the conversation.

"Uh, Gina, you're crushing me."

My teeth brushed against the flesh of his neck, just barely scraping the surface and strengthening the heady scent of blood until it clouded my mind.

Bobby pulled away. "We've got to get you something to eat."

I looked at him and jumped back, like half a body length. In his eyes, I could see the brick of the building directly behind me, the flaking mortar, even the melon-rind moon peeking over its roof... everything but *me*.

"Oh, God!" I wailed.

"What?" Bobby reached out to me. "Gina, what is it? Are you hurt?"

"I don't have a reflection!"

His brows lowered in confusion. "Well, no, it kind of goes with the transformation."

"But no image—don't you get it? How am I supposed to do my hair? What about makeup? I'll poke myself in the eye trying to put on liner."

Bobby looked at me like maybe I had maggots in my hair after all. "Gina, you look *fine*. Better than fine. I don't get—"

"You're right," I said, thinking feverishly. "I do need a bite to eat. And I know just the thing."

Based on how quickly he stepped back, I'm pretty sure he thought I meant him, but that wasn't it. Mom and Dad had been big with the child-rearing clichés. *When life gives you lemons, you make lemonade* had been a favorite of theirs, and I guess it must have sunk in a little. All I needed was a place to shower and change, a stylist, a mani-pedi, and some skin cream and I'd be as good as new. I could even start my own entourage for touch-ups. Better than any mirror. I tried to believe it.

"Not you, dummy," I told him. "*Shirl.*"

"Who?"

"My stylist. I can't go through life looking like this!"

Bobby's brow furrowed further. If he kept that up, vampire or not, he might be needing Botox treatments of his own in a decade or two. "But, um, three's kind of a crowd, don't you think?"

"Oh, so since you're my, what, sire, you get me all to yourself?"

"No, Gina, it's just—"

"Or maybe I should stay a walking disaster so no one else will want me?"

"No, I—"

"No? Good. Then let's go."

Bobby threw his hands into the air, which I caught out of the corner of my eye as I turned to lead the way.

I looked "*fine*"? I snorted to myself. That was, like, the kiss of death. With persuasive powers like that, it was a wonder Bobby had ever made the debate team, let alone been chosen captain.

3

I didn't actually need to breathe, but I'd once heard that it was calming, so I gave it my best shot. In through the nose, out through the mouth. Nope, superpowers aside, I was still up a creek without a paddle—or, way scarier, in the wilds of Neiman Marcus without a credit card. Half the school had probably turned out for my funeral and now remembered me in memoriam as a complete fashion disaster. Tina, my arch-nemesis, was probably overjoyed. No doubt she'd instantly moved in to console Chaz, who'd probably lived through the whole accident without a scratch on him. I needed to stage a comeback. It had to be something big and bold—so fabulous that it mental-flossed away the horrific images of my death. Something like … graduation.

Before my death, I'd worked and slaved for an entire shopping day, hitting every store in a three-town radius to find the perfect dress and matching nail polish. Come hell or bad hair day, I was going to find a way to walk down that aisle. I'd blind my classmates with cosmetic science—no matter how much sunscreen it took. It was practically a public service. And to restore my former fabulosity, I needed Shirl.

Her place, Film Clips, was in the middle of a strip mall toward the center of town. Old movie posters, oversized mirrors ringed with bare bulbs, and film-reel wallpaper made you feel like a star there. Recent pictures of actors and actresses were taped here and there for inspiration. My haircut made me look like a dark Paris Hilton with really awesome volumizer (minus the pocket pup, which was just a distraction from the main attraction).

After being mistaken for body snatchers, Bobby and I were very careful to avoid any police patrols or even street-lights on the way to Clips. Trying not to be noticed was new for me. It felt so … so … *Mission Impossible*, the theme to which Bobby felt compelled to hum under his breath. We now crouched behind one of only three vehicles in the strip mall lot, the one closest to Clips. The other two were way down at the end—one a nondescript van backed up to the open doors of a sporting goods store, and the other a dark sedan sitting low to the ground. Of course, *our* hiding spot was a completely grody rustbucket of a car that looked like someone had driven it to hell and back and forgotten to hose off the ick. I couldn't even steady myself on the door for fear of tetanus or something.

Bobby had parked his own rattletrap down the block, rather than in the strip mall's parking lot, so that it wouldn't be connected with Shirl's upcoming disappearance. He still wasn't thrilled about the idea of turning her, but had caved when I told him the alternative was putting *him* through cosmetology school to take Shirl's place.

I peered over the rustbucket's hood and into Clips to do some, like, visual recon. Next to me, Bobby did the same. Sure enough, Shirl was alone in there, singing along to some song on her radio and...Oh. My. God. With no rhythm whatsoever, she was popping hips, shimmying things that continued jigging once she'd jogged, and using the broom alternately as a dance partner and a microphone. She looked like someone had dumped fire ants down her pants.

"*What* is she doing?" Bobby asked.

My thoughts exactly. My upper lip curled. "I know. It's totally embarrassing. Almost enough to make me abort the mission and find a new stylist."

Bobby looked at me. "Over bad sweeping technique?"

I stared back in disbelief. "Over the really heinous shimmy-dance she's doing with that broom. She looks like a spaz. God, you are such a geek."

Bobby blinked. "But she's just pushing the hair around."

I rolled my eyes heavenward. "I rest my case."

But my hunger didn't give a damn about dignity or shimmy dances. The roar of bloodlust chased out all other thoughts, and made my stomach cramp and my knees weak. The thought of my teeth breaking through the surface of Shirl's skin, spilling blood like hot nectar into my mouth, nearly knocked me over for the second time that night. I actually forgot myself enough that I put a steadying hand on the rustbucket.

"You all right?" Bobby asked.

What the hell. I had my geek—I'd add the spaz, and all I'd need was a dweeb to collect the whole set.

A door whipped open at the other end of the strip, followed by the sharp crack of something heavy smacking the pavement.

"Ow! Watch what you're doing, lamebrain!" a voice called out. I would have looked anyway, but there was something familiar about that voice . . .

"You'll heal," answered a woman, not sounding particularly excited about the idea.

Bobby elbowed me in the ribs. "That can't be . . . Larry Pearce?"

"Who?" I asked. I looked over, but I didn't recognize the flame-haired guy with the envy-inspiring complexion totally made for exfoliant commercials. The guy next to him, though . . . him I knew. Rick Lopez. No wonder the voice had sounded so familiar. Between my new vamp senses and the strip mall security lights, there was no mistaking the steroid-enhanced build, blue and gold varsity jacket, and beady little eyes of Chaz's wingman—and fullback or hatchback or something for the Mozulla High Lemurs. And there was some kind of she-hulk with them, helping to wrestle duffle bags worth of gear out the doors.

I didn't know what to process first. "Why can't it be Larry?" I whispered at Bobby.

"He's dead," he whispered back.

My lips twitched. "So are we."

"Yeah, but—"

"What?"

"I don't know, it's just weird. And I don't think they're paying for that stuff," he added, jutting his chin at the *Closed* sign.

Another poster boy for steroid abuse got out of the van and opened the back doors for their haul, but he wasn't looking around for patrols or even at what he was doing. His eyes were totally stroking the curves of Chickzilla's unitard. And what was with the unitard, anyhow? There was a reason those had gone the way of the dinosaurs—or should have, anyway. If you're not clear on why, I have one word for you: access. Or two more: potty break. Think about it.

"Shouldn't we stop them?" Bobby hissed.

It didn't really seem like our job, but I was itching to try out my mod new bod. The problem was that we were outnumbered, and I didn't know how many of them were vamps like us. Rick had a zit on his chin that made me think he wasn't part of any fanged fraternity (not after seeing Larry's porcelain perfection), but I didn't know about the others. And I doubted the bulgy things in the bags were as harmless as fishing lures and night crawlers.

"Stop them how? Fight? Or, like, call the cops and wait to testify?" I asked. It was totally sweet that he wanted to go all hero, but someone had to be the voice of reason. "We're not exactly—"

The lights went out in Film Clips. Shirl was on the move.

"Go, go, go!" I called, voice rising as I pushed Bobby into action.

Shirl had her back to us as she locked up, but she whirled at the sound of our footfalls (neither Bobby nor I had mastered the cat-like grace that movie vamps always seem to have). Her eyes widened as she spotted me.

"G-G-Gina!"

It was all I could do not to snort. The stuttering-in-fear thing was such a cliché, although the trembling, deer-in-headlights look was a nice touch.

"Shhh," I soothed, not wanting Rick to overhear and word of my rising to get around school before I staged my comeback.

"The rumors of her death have been greatly exaggerated," Bobby put in helpfully.

"But I went to the funeral," Shirl said, her green eyes never leaving my golden-brown.

See, I just knew Shirl was a gem. I wondered if there was any chance my parents had gotten her to do my hair for the viewing. If not, all it must have done was lie there and be square. And the *whole school* would have seen me that way. I wondered if my reputation would ever recover.

"Shirl, that was, uh, mistaken identity," I improvised. I couldn't turn her right there with potential witnesses looking on; I needed to come up with a story, but quick. "You have to come with me. Help … help me change my look! It was all a conspiracy, and I'm still in danger."

I could feel the fear rolling off her in waves and could tell she wasn't buying it. Probably the lisp brought on by my pointy new teeth made me sound sinister. But her fear felt good. Eerily good. I felt like a kitten with a catnip ball.

"Hey!" Rick yelled, loud enough to spin me around. His gaze met mine, even down the length of the mall, and I wondered whether he had really good eyes or if my voice had carried. "You!"

Shirl was there one second, gone the next, taking advantage of my distraction to bolt toward the rustbucket.

"Damn! After her!" I hollered at Bobby.

Shirl was in her car, with the door slammed and the motor running, before we could do a thing. I stood in front of it, but she just backed up and peeled out.

"What *about* me?" I asked, rounding on Rick, ready

to accept him as a substitute blood donor. But all I caught were the tail lights of the van. Rick and his compatriots had fled, the dark sedan leading the way. The shop doors thumped shut behind them.

"Uh, Bobby, what did you give me—cooties?"

4

I stumbled twice on my way to Bobby's POS rattletrap, feeling like I did during that grapefruit diet I'd tried for prom season—cranky and faint.

"You couldn't have knocked over a butcher shop on the way to pick me up?" I snapped at him.

"Knocked over?"

"You know, broke and entered, held up, robbed." He looked like I'd stunned him with a clue-by-four. "Wait, you really do have a receipt for those clothes, don't you?" I asked.

"Well, yeah," he said, like it was obvious. And of course it was. Bobby, chess champ and debate team captain, was white-knight material. This living-outside-the-system thing was probably going to kill him all over again.

My voice softened. "Bobby, you're *dead*."

"Yeah, but they don't know that. My credit's still good."

"How? No, I'll get to that in a minute. What I mean is, we're, like, beyond the law. Renegades, right? No reflection, so probably no image left behind on pesky security cameras."

"Yeah, I guess, but stealing is *wrong*."

Bobby opened the car door for me, every bit like his red-orange Crown Vic was some kind of chariot. I could practically taste the blood beneath his skin as I passed him. It would be warm and moist and . . . I licked my lips in anticipation.

"Focus," Bobby said, eying me like I might spring on him at any moment.

I was focused—on the smooth curve of his neck, the pulse point—which, now that I looked closely, wasn't actually pulsing. Totally weird. What were we talking about?

"Stealing, wrong," Bobby prompted.

That brought my attention up to his eyes. "Do you have a job?" I asked.

Bobby paused in the act of tucking me into the car and closing my door. "Not any more. The comic shop doesn't have too many evening hours."

My eyes rolled. "Well then, didn't you just transfer your credit card debts from the store to your parents?"

He was totally dumbstruck. I air-scored a point to me.

"And what do you mean, 'they don't know' you're dead?" I asked.

Bobby finally closed my door and got himself settled into the driver's seat. He waited for the car to choke and catch before answering. "Um, well, I kinda just passed out somewhere and woke up a couple days later. No one ever found me."

"You dog." I punched his arm. "Passed out as in partied too hard?"

"Yeah, sorta. So where to?" Bobby put the car into gear, but left his foot firmly on the brake. It seemed a little late for *follow that car*, though I did worry about what Rick and his buddies had been up to. Did Rick know he was hanging out with a dead guy? What was in the sacks? Were they just removing all of our town's potential wooden-stake launchers, like crossbows and such? I couldn't imagine we had many. Or were they stocking up? Were they planning on going a-huntin'? And for who? Not that it was any of my business.

"How'd you die?" I asked Bobby, looking for something to distract me from the gnawing in my belly and all the questions I had no way to answer. "And—wait—when did you get all vamped out?"

Bobby made an inarticulate sound of frustration and hit the gas with more force than necessary, jerking us forward. "What do you think Larry was up to with those guys?" he countered, echoing my thoughts.

"Stop trying to change the subject. How and when?"

He shot me a look. "*Fine,*" he huffed. "It happened when the debate team was celebrating our win over Baldaiga. One of the guys scored some fake IDs..."

"Uh-huh," I encouraged.

"So we kinda got a little, um, toasted, and there was this woman—"

"Yes," I prompted, intrigued.

"And she was all, you know... and we got kind of, um, friendly. Then, I guess anemia and alcohol or whatever kinda finished me. I wandered off somewhere, found a nice quiet spot where the light didn't hurt my eyes, and sorta passed on."

With my super vamp senses, I could see him flush red, the color starting at the tips of his ears and running over his face to creep down his neck. It was cute, in a completely geeky sort of way. Bobby seemed like such a rule guy that it couldn't have been easy for his friends to convince him to cut loose for a night. It was going to be even harder now to convince him to take risks, since the last one led to his unlife, but I'd always liked a challenge.

"So you scored a victory and a vamp," I encouraged. "Go you."

Bobby cut a glance my way. "You say it like she was some kind of prize."

I shrugged. "Most guys would think so."

But I was starting to get the picture that Bobby wasn't "most guys," at least not the ones I'd hung out with. I knew what *they* wanted when they opened a car door for me—a glimpse of thigh when my skirt rode up. But I didn't know what to do with a gentleman. I kind of thought they'd gone out with corsets and bustles. It made me feel sort of…wobbly, like Bobby was a pair of heels that didn't quite fit but were just too adorable to pass up.

"Where are we going?" I asked, suddenly realizing I'd never given him a directive, and yet we were underway.

"The Galleria, I guess. Good place to get a bite this time of night. Should be just about closing."

I looked at him in horror, then down at the totally dirt-stained atrocity my parents had chosen to bury me in. It was a really good thing I'd saved the bag with all the clothes. I launched into the back seat and dug in.

"I'm changing. Don't peek," I ordered.

Bobby swerved. "But—but I'm just talking about grabbing someone on the way to her car."

"I might see someone I know!" He totally didn't get it. Oh God, Rick had already seen me looking like a train wreck. By tomorrow it would be all over school—not that anyone would believe him, of course, or that I'd be there to take the ribbing. "You got any, like, wet wipes and maybe a brush?"

5

I woke the next night like someone had goosed me with a taser, flailing and fighting and totally trapped! There was a weight, an arm bearing me down, and then someone shouting in my ear. "Calm down, Gina. Calm. It's just me. Full dark will hit you like that at first. Shhh!"

It took me a minute to make out the words and even longer for the streetlight bleeding through my shades to put things into focus. I was in my own room—my parents having flown as predicted to some exotic location to wash away the discomfort of my death. Bobby'd wanted to go to his Greg Brady–style bachelor pad, conveniently located over his parents' garage, but his parents, not knowing he was dead, had been lurking around to do an intervention and get him back on track, which meant classes and sunlight and other unhealthy things.

My house was silent as a grave except for Bobby talking to me like he was some horse whisperer and I was a spooked filly. I forced my eyes to stop rolling in panic, and focused on the familiar—the lavender sheets twisted around me, the deep purple coverlet pushed to the foot of my bed, one fuzzy raspberry pillow buried in the sheets and the others fallen to the floor ... and Fluffy, the Creamsicle-colored stuffed cat I'd had for as long as I could remember. Without a thought, I reached out to grab Fluffy and hug him to me. I wondered what Bobby made of it, but I didn't want to turn and see pity or whatever in his eyes. One of his arms was still around me; the other hand stroked my hair. I tried to relax into it, but I was freaked. I'd lost time. Between sunrise and sunset was ... nothing. No dreams, no rolling over to find a better position. Just, like, sudden death.

For some reason it hit me—as it hadn't fully, before—that my old life was truly gone. I'd missed some finals already, and would miss more. Without, like, divine inspiration and an extreme makeover, my diploma was nothing but a pipe dream—and after all the effort I'd taken to cheat off Marissa's French tests and actually study for Math 12. I'd never again mock Mr. Collins' bad rug with

Becca and Marcy or ogle the butts of the football team as they did their pre-game stretches. If I'd been human I would have hyperventilated. But I wasn't...not anymore.

I held on to Fluffy for dear life and snuggled against Bobby, as a cue to keep on doing what he was doing.

Eventually, Bobby's soothing did the trick and the knife-edge of panic slipped away. *I could get used to this*, I thought, nearly bringing back the blinding fear. Boys were fickle, and my parents had pretty much taught me to rely on myself alone. Somehow, Bobby had just kind of snuck up under my defenses with his tenderness and white-knighthood. Made me want to trust. I stiffened right up at the thought and Bobby paused in his stroking, giving me the perfect cue to throw off his arm and the covers and rise from the bed.

My feet thumped as they hit the floor, making me realize that I was still in the knee-high boots I'd nabbed at the mall along with my bite to eat. My sassy new mini-skirt and red pirate blouse were now so horribly wrinkled that I couldn't be seen in them, not even by Bobby unless I decided to scare him off. I remembered the after-prom party where we'd hooked up, the feel of his teeth on my neck...

"Don't look," I ordered him, quickly grabbing a hot pink cami from my closet to replace the wrinkled pirate blouse. At least I'd be partially presentable.

"Why?" he asked, sounding honestly baffled.

"Because I said so."

I did a quick change with my back to him, all the while wondering if there'd been some kind of hypnotic power to his bite that was making me go all soft and dreamy, making me forget myself. Yeah, that was probably it. The hottie I'd ambushed at the mall on the way to his car had gone all dreamy-eyed when I bit him, after the initial protest and attempt to run. Then had come the high of a successful hunt, the hot rush of his blood...mmm. I'd left him passed out in the front seat of his Civic, but smiling, which was a totally weird side-effect.

My vamp-boy rubbed sleep out of his eyes as he ignored my order and watched me pace the room—from my completely hot *Pirates of the Caribbean* poster, to a concert still of Su Surrus, to a group shot of the Baden Boys. I should have ditched that last one, since I was so over them, but the backdrop totally picked up the purple in my wallpaper border and bedspread.

"So, what's our plan?" Bobby asked.

"You're a morning person, aren't you?" I asked, whirling on him for no particular reason.

"Well, *night* now." My lips rose in a snarl. "Anyway," he continued quickly, "we can't just hide out here forever."

"You want a plan? We need to stage a comeback. You're damn right that we can't keep scrounging mall meals and hiding out. We're *vamps!* Top of the food chain and all that. We need to make some kind of splash. I'm thinking we crash graduation." And I knew just the set of wheels to get us there—a chariot rather than a rattletrap like Bobby's POS. If

Chaz's cherry-red sportster had survived the accident and the muscle car that ran us off the road—and if Chaz himself had survived—I could get revenge on my ex and get a hot new set of wheels in a single act of grand theft auto.

Bobby blinked. "Crash graduation? I'm talking seriously."

"So am I."

Outside, something went crash-bang and I whirled toward the sound as if I could see through walls. It sounded like one of the decorative flower pots my mother kept on the front porch.

"I thought your folks were gone," Bobby hissed, his voice now barely above a whisper. He was already rising from the bed, searching for the shoes he'd had time to kick off, unlike me who'd been totally ambushed by the sunrise.

"They are. They have to be … " because no way would they risk countering their Botox treatments—their faces might crack. "Let's check it out." I was flooded with purpose. "Maybe it's a burglar and we can have some fun."

Bobby looked at me like I'd lost my mind, but I was getting used to that.

"Come on," I insisted.

I was out of the room and halfway down the stairs before he could protest, not that it would have done him any good.

"I don't hear anything now," Bobby whispered.

Neither did I, unless I counted the creaking of the staircase close behind me. "Keep toward the railing and walk on the blades of your feet," I instructed him.

"You've done this before?"

I refused to answer on the grounds that it might incriminate me. Besides, if *"this"* meant catching burglars in the act, the answer was no. If it meant sneaking out . . . "The sound came from around front," I said instead. "We'll go out the back door and circle around behind them."

"What if they're coming in one way while we're going out the other?"

"Jeez, Bobby. First you think no one's here, now you're afraid we'll miss them. Make up your mind."

I stopped Bobby's eye roll with a light elbow to the gut, causing him to "oof."

"Follow me," I ordered.

I led him through the kitchen, all silent and pristine, and put my ear to the back door. Nothing. Or maybe a little wind and some rustling leaves, but nothing special.

"You ready?" I asked, feeling him move up behind me. "Go."

I turned the lock, threw the door open, and bolted through it, a reprise of the *Mission Impossible* theme song running through my head.

Pain registered before the pressure. Something grabbed my arm and twisted. Blunt force smashed me up against the wall of the house, my cheek scraping on the fake Tudor stucco.

"Ouch!" I yelled.

"Hey, let—" Bobby's cry was cut off by the thump of more flesh on stucco.

The smell of something really foul, like beef jerky and cheap beer, nearly made me gag.

"Shut up," a voice ordered, low and mannish and the source of those fumes. "Mellisande wants to talk to you two."

"Who?" I asked.

Bobby moaned.

The owner of the jerky breath wrenched my arms up and my shoulders shrieked in pain as my blades tried to meet in the middle of my back. Something was slipped around my wrists and pulled tight before I could even process it enough to react. Only once my hands were trapped did the weight against my back ease.

I whirled around to face Chickzilla—the same bulgy bimbo I'd seen lugging the bags with Rick Lopez last night. Bobby was getting pinned and zip-tied by some thug built like a hydrant—low to the ground and rock-solid—with scary amounts of hair bursting out of the collar of his wifebeater T-shirt.

Larry and another thug came running from around the front of the house.

"Piece of cake," Chickzilla announced.

"Oh, man, I missed all the action," Larry protested.

"Later. You have all eternity," the Chick said with a twist of her lips, like maybe *she* didn't.

She did, however, have the joy of manhandling me toward some waiting cars, one the sedan from the strip mall and the other a matte green muscle car...with a nearly caved in wheel well and a long scrape along the side.

It was the last thing I remembered seeing before waking in my coffin.

I stopped short and the Chick crashed into me, almost knocking me to the ground.

"That car," I said, ignoring her attempt to budge me again. "*You're* the reason I'm dead!"

A blow fell right between my poor abused shoulder blades, propelling me forward again.

"Oh, was that you?" asked the thug who hadn't yet had the pleasure of smacking us around.

He didn't sound the least bit sorry, but he would be. I turned to memorize his face, which wasn't hard. Though he had similar bulges, he had half a foot on Sparky, as I'd decided to call the hydrant-shaped guy (since "Hydrant" just made me think of peeing dogs). Not-Sparky had a hawklike, down-turned nose and a prominent, upturned chin that were trying to meet in the middle of his face. It was not a good look.

Bobby's silence through all of this seemed nearly inhuman, and I was about ready to explode on him when the thugs plus Larry threw us into the back seat of the sedan and set the child locks. Larry and Hawkman, as I'd dubbed my killer, folded themselves into the muscle car, which looked like it had been a sweet ride before nudging me over to the dark side. A Charger, I thought, proud of having picked up something from all the time wasted listening to Chaz and his friends froth at the mouth over cars, video games, and football stats.

I landed with my head on Bobby's lap and quickly righted myself—as best I could with my bound hands. "Who the hell is Mellisande?" I asked him.

"I'm totally sorry," Bobby whispered, as if Chickzilla and her cohort couldn't hear him from one seat away.

"About *what?*"

"Well, see, you and I weren't together then."

Boys. "Wait, Mellisande's the vamp from after the debate, the one you—"

"Yeah, I think so. I don't know what I did to piss her off. I don't even think I gave her my real name."

"Shut up back there," Sparky barked.

"Why? It's not like we're plotting. You can hear us just fine," I snapped back.

"Because I said so."

"*What*ever." My hands instinctively tried to come forward to form the "W" sign, but the twist-tie thingies brought them up short, giving my poor, abused shoulders another twinge.

"Look," Chickzilla said. "Rick and Larry recognized you two last night. And since you," she twitched in my general direction, "are supposed to be dead, and you," a second twitch at Bobby, "*aren't*—as far as we knew, anyway—blue eyes here has some explaining to do. End. Of. Story."

I glared daggers at our captors and we drove in silence for a while, until I couldn't stand it any more.

"You must have made quite an impression," I said to Bobby.

He gave me one of those smiles that convinced me he had some typical male in him after all. "Guess so."

Sparky hissed.

"No one was talking to you," I told him.

"No one should be talking, period."

"Napoleon complex," I whispered to Bobby. Then louder, "Hey, you know you've got some male-pattern baldness starting back here?"

Chickzilla chuckled and Sparky started to veer toward the shoulder of the road before she nudged him back on track. "Just drive. I don't think Mellisande wants this one, so you can probably do whatever you want once she's done, but she'll be pissed if you take the initiative without her say-so."

I didn't like the sound of that. I looked at Bobby to see if he was going to pipe up, but he seemed totally focused inward, like he was trying to be some kind of Zen master … a Zen master with ants in his pants, the way he was squirming around. I didn't know what his hands were doing there behind his back, but—

Bobby suddenly nestled up against me and I felt his hands scrabble at my waistband.

"Hey."

"Shhh!" he hissed.

"What's going on back there?" Chickzilla asked.

"Bobby bumped me," I offered, though I still didn't know what I was covering for.

"Don't make me pull this car over," Sparky threatened.

Something cold and hard pressed into my hand, and I started before I realized that Bobby was trying to pass me something. I grabbed hold of what felt like a Swiss Army Knife, and he gave a tug, as if to free one of the tools. Then he scooched until his wrists were beneath my hands, which I guess meant I was supposed to saw him loose.

He winced as I moved the blade back and forth over what I hoped was the restraint but maybe wasn't. The thing—knife—jerked in my hands with every swipe, and I strained to hold on in my awkward position. The car hit a pothole, Bobby yelped, and I lost hold of the knife.

Bobby let his head smack back against the seat. "Great," he muttered.

I felt around on the seat for the dropped knife and only succeeded in pushing it farther into the crevice.

"Sorry," I whispered.

After only a second, Bobby whispered, "Never liked that knife anyway. Been thinking of upgrading."

I smiled—feebly, because that's all it deserved. Still, I appreciated that he'd made an attempt at a joke, especially after I'd fumbled our chance at escape.

6

ellisande's digs were a thing of beauty. All clean, modern lines and mirrored windows that I was guessing protected the vamps within and foiled prying eyes from without. And it was... maybe not huge, but ginormous at the very least.

I was still trying to figure out the mixed bag of bodies we'd seen so far. Larry had to be a vamp, since Bobby knew him to be dead, but everything about him said newbie. Chickzilla had the power to smack us around, but she didn't seem to be one of us. Sparky just wasn't pretty enough to be a vamp. Hawkman ... I hadn't seen enough of him to be sure. He wasn't *Top Model* material for certain, but maybe the transformation could only do so much. Anyway, it was clear that this Mellisande chick had at least some human minions, which made sense if daylight smacked her around the way it did me. She couldn't let herself be helpless and unguarded from sun-up to sundown. Minions sounded pretty cool, maybe even cooler than a mere entourage.

I didn't get much chance to mull all that over, since Bobby and I were being hustled through a low-lit entryway that nonetheless gave an impression of space (or at least height). We were pushed into a back room with heavy, dark gold drapes and lamps and such in a style I think they call "Missionary" or something like that. Everything was all light-wood frames filled in with rectangles, triangles, and circles of stained glass in earthy tones, like the artist only had elementary school skills and a natural palette to work with. It still managed to be cool, I guess, in that monied, understated kind of way.

The lady herself rose from behind an impressive desk as we entered, leaving the hottie who'd been leaning over her in mid-sentence. I sized up the competition as she practically floated toward us like a finishing-school diva. A cornflower blue silk dress crisscrossed low over her chest, spilling cleavage and yet still managing to look classy. The skirt portion had just enough fabric to levitate as she glided, revealing *way* too much leg. I looked down at the bed-wrinkled skirt I hadn't gotten to change and then at Bobby, whose gaze hadn't yet risen above Mellisande's mid-thigh. She smirked at me as I turned back toward her. Above the neckline she was all Kewpie-doll cute. Bowed lips, pert nose, wavy honey-blond hair, eyes the exact same shade as her dress. I hated her on sight.

I snarled and turned to study the much more intriguing hottie she'd left behind. Unlike most of the minions I'd seen, this one wasn't bulgy at all, or not so you'd notice. Bobby's blushing must have been infectious, 'cause as I met the man's rare green eyes—I mean, like, gemstone green—I felt a little flush. And that *hair*... bad-boy long, black as midnight, falling just slightly in his face, making me want to brush it back. I felt like I was falling into a dream of firelight and hot toddies, whatever they were, bearskin rugs, and—

I blinked, snapping myself out of the bizarre little PG-13 film playing in my head. I mean, bearskin rugs were so yesterday. Not to mention, I ... I froze as pretty boy pulled out a desk drawer, probably to put back the document he'd been holding, and a deep blue glow emerged, bathing his face in light.

I must have made a sound, or maybe it was the fixed look on my face, but the darling diva turned and saw the scene for herself. Her eyes widened and for a sec her polish and control fell away for something like wonder. Then she shut it down.

"Connor," she barked. "Bring it here."

"But it shouldn't be poss—"

"Connor!"

The look he shot her was venomous, but he palmed whatever was in the drawer, light leaking out from between his fingers, and walked toward us. I probably should have been scared, but I'd seen Connor both stare into it and lift it with his bare hands, so I figured it wasn't going to incinerate us on contact. And besides, I was way too curious for caution. Just forty-eight hours ago I'd had no idea that vamps and unidentified glowing objects even existed. I felt a little like Alice in Wonderland—with pointy teeth and bloodlust. Okay, so maybe as Quentin Tarantino would do Alice…

The blazing gemstone, and I could now see that's what it was, moved toward us, even more riveting than the hottie's eyes. In fact, it shone the same impossible color as Bobby's baby blues, and it flared as it neared him, as if like called to like.

"I knew it," Mellisande gasped, but if that was true, why did she seem so surprised? "Try the girl," she added, turning her narrowed eyes on me.

Connor held the glow out toward me, putting himself between me and Bobby as a buffer. The gemstone flared once, and then faded almost to nothing. I was disappointed without even knowing why.

"Dim—what a surprise," Mellisande said nastily. "Remove the girl."

"You won't hurt her!" Bobby cried out, sounding credibly commanding. The gemstone flared again, nearly blinding me, but at the same time it was *pretty*, like the sun. It would make a fabulous conversation piece in the right setting.

Mellisande's and Connor's eyes met and something passed between them. Then Mellisande wet her lips seductively and turned to Bobby, holding her hand up to pause the scene just as Chickzilla started to lead me away.

"She means something to you, this cheap … thing?"

Bobby broke from her spell long enough to look at me. "Yes." The heart I wasn't using anyway kinda melted.

Mellisande's nose wrinkled in distaste. "*Really?* Well, that's … interesting. You and I have unfinished business. Perhaps I will hold her as collateral for your good behavior." She flicked her hand, as if hitting *restart*, and Chickzilla led me away, painfully gripping my elbow.

One of the other thugs flanked me, leaving two behind with Bobby and his vampire vixen. If steam could really come out of ears, my whistle would be blowing.

7

A bazillion hours passed and Bobby didn't even come visit me in my dungeon. Not that it was a dungeon exactly. I mean, this was Ohio. And I could hear a constant murmur of voices from somewhere, like a radio turned too low to make out the words, so the walls couldn't be all that thick. But it was desperately dim and dusty—a partitioned-off section of basement with a cot, a door inset with bars, and a truly gag-worthy topless toilet. It stank like way too many people had tried hovering over the pot and missed.

Personally, I was hoping to die a true death before things got that urgent for me.

As a distraction, my brain kept supplying images of just what 'ole Melli could want with *my* boyfriend. I wondered what kind of unfinished business she could be talking about and whether there was anything Bobby hadn't told me about that post-debate fling with his dam, or whatever she'd be called in vamp lingo. But duplicity didn't seem to be in Bobby's makeup. He was almost absurdly noble—though really, how well did I know him? We'd been practically speed dating.

I'd already tried to turn into a bat or mist or *anything* that would help me escape, but either fiction had things all wrong or I wasn't doing it right. I seriously needed to get my hands on *Vampirism for Dummies*, the *CliffsNotes* version, or maybe a subscription to *Modern Goth*. With my escape plan, such as it was, shot, I was reduced to counting the concrete blocks of my cell and developing extreme makeover ideas for the pitiful place when the basement door creaked open.

"Bobby!" I called, rising from the cot, fluffing up some parts of me and smoothing down others as I approached the barred door so I could see better.

But the guy who'd entered the basement was none other than Rick-the-rat-Lopez, who was partially responsible for me being in this dump.

"Traitor," I said, too ladylike to spit.

Rick leaned against the closed door and gave me a

kind of creepy grin. "Can't be a traitor. I'd have to stand for something first."

"Fine. Rat, sleaze, doofus—take your pick."

He gave me one of those up and down looks guys seem to think are suave. "I don't think you want to talk to me like that, Gina. We're not in high school anymore. No more Chaz, no more primping posse. Just you and me— and I'm the one with the power...and the key. You play your cards right, maybe we can help each other out."

I didn't like the glint in his eye or the way his hand was kneading itself on his thigh, perilously close to—ewww! It was on the tip of my tongue to ask just how desperate he was that he needed to trade for favors, especially since I had to look like something the cat dragged in and batted around. But it didn't seem too bright to drive away my only source of information, and possibly of escape.

"We might be able to come to an arrangement," I hedged, sidling up to the bars and tamping down my gag reflex. "What does this Melli witch want with me and Bobby?"

"I didn't come to talk about Bobby."

I gave a cute little pout and added a nose wrinkle for good measure. "Come on. You gave us up. How do I know I can trust you? You've got to give me something."

Rick got closer, close enough to try to look down my blouse, but I shied away with a squeak when he slipped a hand through the bars.

"Shhh!" he warned, which was interesting. It meant

that help was pretty close by, maybe even as close as those voices I'd heard earlier—

"You want ... something," I said, shuddering to think what that was. "I want something too. Answers."

Rick's eyes narrowed, so I took a *deep* breath to distract him from the suspicion that I might be playing him. It had the usual effect of inflating my chest and riveting any man in the vicinity. Remembering to breathe took a bit of practice, but it sure got results.

"You want answers? Fine." He spat the word out, not even bothering to lift his gaze to mine again as he spoke. "Here's what ticks me off. Mellisande turns herself a vamp army. Even nerds like Bobby and Larry have a place in her new world order, but does she remember us baseline humans, as she calls us? Oh no—we're too useful. She likes us just the way we are. Well, screw that. I'm branching out. So, here's the deal: you bite me, I free you. We both win. If Larry hadn't been there last night, we'd never have had to go through this little dance. I'd have kept you to myself and tracked you down later. He's the one you should be pissed at."

I considered that. It sounded good—in theory. One bite and I could sashay out of here, assuming Rick really could get me out of the house and not just this damned cell, but it felt ... wrong. What was I going to do on the outside? Either I could live forever in the shadows or out myself. Assuming I could avoid any righteous mobs convinced I was evil incarnate, maybe I could spin fifteen minutes of fame out of my rising. But if fame were fickle? If the cameras didn't love me—or even capture me on film? What then? Flipping burgers? Working retail? Okay, that wouldn't be bad as far as employee discounts went, but then there was the actual customer service. And escape would mean leaving Bobby. Running off with—gag me with a celery stalk—Rick. Maybe I should stick around long enough to see if I could make a place for myself in Melli's "new world order." Just as, like, a jumping off point for launching my own empire. First, though, I'd have to get out of this cell. Maybe escaping on my own terms would show her what I was made of.

"I don't know," I hedged. "Maybe I should see what the other side is offering first."

His leer went a bit feral. "Nothing good. Mellisande's got some kind of plans for your new stud, but for you? You're like the red-headed stepchild. And with Mellisande, if you're not one of hers, you're no one. She keeps her people on a pretty tight leash."

"Like you?"

He snarled. "Fine. If you won't come willingly—"

He leapt for the cell door, key out like he was ready to stab me, but just happened to hit the keyhole instead. The door swung open, and I nearly crowed. Oh, I jumped back out of the way like some scared little girly-girl, but just far enough to put some real momentum behind the swing of my pointy-toed boot. I had Rick doubled over the family jewels before he knew what hit him.

"Gotcha!" I hooted, swooping down to grab the key. Only he still had enough presence of mind to grab my wrist, fast as thought, and *twist*, bringing me down onto one knee in front of him. I didn't like the position one bit and before any qualms could take root, I head-butted him dead center. *This* time he really went down, howling and cursing. But his diction sucked, so I couldn't tell which hell he'd see me in.

I grabbed the key and stepped over his writhing body to make my escape, locking the cell door behind me with Rick-the-rat on the inside.

I was in a cinderblock hallway, like Melli had finished her basement on the cheap. It echoed, so the murmur of voices bounced around, but they seemed to be coming from a set of double doors off to my right. I made for them and burst through—straight into the Twilight Zone.

The scene inside stopped me dead … well, immobile, anyway. A few eerily familiar people near the doors turned in surprise at my sudden entrance … and then I was hit with a flying tackle, like a blast from the past.

"Gina!" a voice shouted in my ear.

"Marcy!" I hugged back for all I was worth. There might have been squealing.

"Oh, Gina, thank God. I thought I was all alone in here."

I looked around at all the people—all the very familiar, very *un*dead bodies which, I was assuming, had gone missing from cemeteries much like the one I'd risen from. Right away I saw Cassandra Stiles, who'd died in some bizarre hot-tub incident a few weeks ago, and an under-classman whose name I couldn't remember who'd suppos-edly OD'd on drugs. Marcy'd still been alive last I knew, so she must have died on prom night like me. This was, like, déjà vu all over again. High school, part two. Rick had mentioned Melli's vamp army, but just how many had the dragon lady killed? I couldn't take it in. All these kids ...

"Becca is still on the other side," Marcy continued, adding to my confusion.

"The other side of what?" I pulled out of the hug far enough to look into my friend's amber eyes. I never thought I'd see them again. Suddenly, I got it. "Oh, you mean she didn't rise?" I asked, horrified.

"She never fell," Marcy whispered, like it was the ulti-mate social faux pas. "She's still got finals and everything, poor girl. But Gina, honey, speaking of poor things, what on earth have they done to you?"

I remembered my wrinkled clothes, my continuing lack of shower or hairbrush. Further proof that my world was spinning out of control.

"Makeover!" we both cried.

8

It was the weirdest thing. I'd never been to prison, but the bizarro-world I'd entered through those double-doors looked like one of those Club Fed kind of places where they kept the shoplifting starlets of the world. It was, like, a dormitory. Boys and girls living together, complete with product and accessories. It was enough to bring tears to my eyes—only when I wiped them away they were more plasma than saline, and it totally skeeved me out.

There were a ton of questions I wanted to ask—from who to how to when. It seemed like a cross-section of

Mozulla High had been drop-kicked into Mellisande's basement. Why in the world? Why kids? Why *us*?

But I didn't get the chance to ask any of my questions, since Marcy quickly found a sink and dunked my head into it, scrubbing my hair to within an inch of its life. I relaxed into it. It was like the light at the end of the tunnel, making me realize I could have my life and cheat it to. Maybe I *didn't* have to crash graduation to get my groove back, though I wasn't giving up on the idea just yet. I still had friends. I wasn't a total misfit, cut off from everything I cared about.

It seemed like all was right with the world ... until Marcy had me fling my sopping wet head up out of the water and I came face to face with my arch nemesis since childhood. And behind her, nasty smirk on his face and hand on her waist, was my ex, Chaz. My non-beating heart sank right to my toes. It just figured that eternal life would come with a catch. Or with two, in this case.

Every girl has an image of how she'd like to face down her ex, and never does it involve looking like a drowned rat. Generally, there's a *Miss Congeniality*–level makeover to be considered, and I was only on step one. But hey, since our breakup was fairly non-traditional, being that it involved separation by death, I guess our reunion fit right in.

Marcy froze when she saw them, but I flung my hair about a few more times, lashing them all with my run-off—even Marcy, who was cruising for a talk about priorities and what constituted need-to-know.

"Look, honey," Tina said with a sneer. "It's night of the living bed-head."

I sneered right back. "Hey, if you'd come up with that on your own, I'd be impressed, but it looks like you get everything second hand." My gaze flicked over to Chaz and then back to the very bane of my existence—bottle-blonder-than-thou Tina Carstairs, with her knock-off designer duds and her warm and fuzzy feelings about other girls' boyfriends. She'd been throwing herself at Chaz for, like, ever, and lucky her, he'd finally made the catch.

Speaking of which, my ex-arm-candy didn't seem any too happy to see me.

"I hear you traded down," Tina continued, not smart enough to realize she was outmatched. "I knew you didn't have any taste, but to go trolling with the chess club..."

I grinned evilly, because, I mean, *come on*. "Have you *seen* Bobby recently?"

There was more to him than spankin' new looks, but I had to put it in terms Tina would understand. Besides, if she knew I was really interested, he'd probably be next on her "to do" list.

Whatever response she was going to make died on her lips as the double doors slammed open.

I was guessing that Rick had been found.

9

Marcy leapt back with a squeak, leaving only Tina to be pushed aside from her position up in my grill. I didn't even have time to appreciate her indignation before two burly beefcakes grabbed my arms in vice-like grips. Yeah, because one beefcake wouldn't have been enough. I could tell by their strength and perfection that at least smelly Melli had shown enough respect to send actual vamps. Thing One had this whole Polynesian-male-model thing cooking for him, and Thing Two looked like the slightly shaggy young professor girls fantasize about, right down to his button-up Oxford shirt and frame-hugging dockers. If I had to be manhandled, at least it was in style.

My first instinct was to fight like the wet cat I resembled, but that went against my new plan, which was to try to make a place for myself. So instead, I whipped my hair back out of my face, lashing the naughty professor's chest and leaving a honking big wet spot across his spiffy white shirt. "I'm ready," I announced.

Thing One and Thing Two exchanged a look of disbelief and tightened up, like my very passivity showed I was up to something. But it was the look on Marcy's face I was worried about. Her eyes had gone as wide as saucers. Far from defending me, she looked like I might be armed and dangerous or have some kind of communicable skin disease. It hurt. I wondered what kind of sweet deal the others had here that she'd react so badly to me causing trouble. I made a mental note to ask—if I was ever allowed back.

"Misunderstanding," I told her. "I'll be back."

Melli's thugs didn't look too sure of that as they dragged me off with them, down the hall and up some stairs, totally ignorant of the realities of walking in a skirt and heels.

"*Slow down*," I ordered. "If I break a leg on these heels, you're gonna end up carrying me."

They ignored that entirely.

For the second time that night I was trapped in Mellinoma's office. Thing One buckled my knees with pressure to the backs, bringing me to the floor. There really was no need to put me on the ground, since I was totally going along with them—unless it was, like, a power thing. And going along was not going to be quite as easy as I'd thought, 'cause now I was spitting mad. And if there was one thing I hated—besides pleather and wannabees like Tina Carstairs—it was biting my tongue.

Kneeling just a few feet away from me was Rick. It looked like he felt a bit differently about the whole thing—about-to-pee-his-pants frightened, in fact. I was betting *he'd* say . . . or not say . . . whatever it took to save his bacon. I wondered what that would be, and whether this was about to become some lame he-said/she-said session, 'cause I wasn't exactly Melli's golden child.

Bobby was still in the office, held back from coming to me by one of Melli's perfectly manicured talons. On Melli's other side stood Connor, looking like maybe things had just gotten interesting.

My eyes narrowed. "Get your hands off my boyfriend," I told the witch. *Crap*, this mouth was going to get me into trouble. How hard could it be to play nice?

But Mellisande ignored me, just as her thugs had. "You've caused quite a bit of trouble already," she began, now stroking Bobby's arm instead of merely gripping it. He shook, oddly, but didn't draw back. I shot him a *look*. If that was the way the cookie crumbled, maybe I should have run off with Rick. The very thought made my lip curl. "Make no mistake. Regardless of how attached this one is to you," she gave Bobby's arm a final squeeze, and I wondered why he didn't snarl at being treated like a piece of meat, "I *will* kill you if you give me any more cause. But first," she turned on Rick, "I want to hear why you were where you weren't supposed to be."

Rick's eyes rolled like he was looking for rescue. "I was just … just … checking on a former classmate. That's all. And she jumped me." The not-making-eye-contact thing screamed "fishy" to me, but of course, I'd been there.

"Rick, *look* at me." Apparently, Melli thought so too. There was some serious extra weight to her words, and Rick's gaze snapped up to hers in the blink of an eye. "*Tell me*," she continued, with that same strange emphasis. My skin pricked with goose bumps. My dripping hair chilling my skin, maybe? But I didn't think so.

"I offered her a deal," he said, all creepy monotone. "Her freedom for my transformation. She said no."

All eyes in the room turned on me. I could even feel the thugs behind me staring in disbelief.

"What?" I asked. "Like I was really going to bite *him?* As if." I thought fast. No way was I bringing Bobby into this after he'd let the witch paw him. "Plus, I'm kind of interested in the setup you've got here. It has certain perks." I gave Connor a wink, just to give Bobby some of his own back.

Mellisande eyed me like a brightly colored bug, pretty but best pinned to a board under glass. "So you think I'll make you a better offer?"

I crossed my arms. "I don't think the competition's very fierce."

"Let me … ungh … talk to her," Bobby said through clenched teeth. I wondered if Melli somehow had him frozen, and *that's* why he was letting her play around. I instantly felt badly about giving Connor that wink, and my blood began to boil.

Melli smiled, and it wasn't a nice one. She looked from Bobby to me, those pearly whites flashing like she was some kind of toothpaste ad with a brilliant punch line.

"You've got five minutes. In return, I expect full cooperation. I can enforce it, as Bobby has just found out, but it'll be so much easier on all of us if I don't have to. If I grow weary, I'll simply take it out on you," she said, spearing me with her gaze, which might have been intimidating if I was, like, six, or if her eyes glowed red—but they stayed that same cornflower blue, which was hard to take seriously.

So I just stared her down. With a snap, she summoned Connor to come with her as she walked toward the door of her office. I saw resentment flare on his face.

"Bring the boy," she called over her shoulder. Rick's guards grabbed him, one on each arm, and hauled him kicking and screaming toward the door.

"What's going to happen to him?" Bobby called suddenly, free of his paralysis and stumbling forward with the unexpected release.

"Not your concern," she answered.

Given the whole looming-threat thing, it wasn't the reunion it could have been, but I still rushed into Bobby's arms. He held me so tightly it was a good thing I didn't need to breathe. After a second, though, he pulled back.

"What was with that wink?"

I winced. "I was just trying to get even because you were letting the dragon lady claw you."

He pulled back even farther so he could see my face. "You were jealous!"

I blushed. "We have five minutes and *this* is what you want to talk about?" I asked.

He had a smug guy-grin on his face. "Well … yeah. That and if you want any freedom around here you're going to have to play nice."

"That *was* me playing nice."

"Oh … um, then I've got to say, you kind of suck at it."

"Thanks."

"Well, I mean—"

"Relax. I know. Meanwhile, do *you* know that your sugar mama has a buttload of our recently deceased classmates hiding out in the basement?"

"Yeah, she sort of said something about that in between crap about party-crashing bimbos and how prophecies ought to come with time stamps. She called it an orientation, but it sounded more like ranting to me."

"Did she say anything about why she's collecting kids?"

"Let me think. Blah blah blah … honored guest … blah blah blah … use my talents … No, I don't think so."

I'm sure my eyes flashed. "Is that how you hear women— *blah blah blah?*"

I could actually see the white all around his eyes. "No, no, just her. *You* I listen to."

"Riiight."

"I do. Remember in tenth grade when you and Tanya and that other girl did the Su Surrus song 'Bite Me' for the spring talent show?"

"The one where Tanya forgot half the moves?"

He nodded. "I bought the video tape. Watched it, listened to it, probably every week for a year."

That was so totally sweet…in a kinda geeky, desperate sort of way.

"And hey, I did all right on those clothes I brought you, right?" he added.

I softened; I mean, I had to throw the poor guy a bone. "Okay, maybe, but if I find out you're glossing me—"

"Hell to pay, right?"

"Totally." I let that sink in before asking, "So, why is Melli-noma giving you the royal treatment? Does it have anything to do with that glowy stone?" I asked.

"Maybe, that and the prophecy."

"You mean the one that ought to come with a time stamp? That's about you?"

"Um, yeah, I think so. Haven't I mentioned it?"

"*No*, I would have remembered."

A bang on the door made me jump, and I figured it was a warning that our time was running out.

"I know it's hard," he continued, "but maybe we should give this thing a shot."

"What about Rick?" I asked, not liking the guy but not loving the idea of what Mellisande might do to him. I remembered Rick saying, "If you're not one of hers, you're no one."

Bobby shrugged. "He got himself into trouble. I guess he can get himself out. Anyway, I don't see what we can do right now but watch and learn. Maybe we can figure out how to use our powers for good."

It was such a Bobby thing to say. And it was what I'd been thinking…more or less, anyway. But despite my resolve, I wasn't sure how long I'd be able to hold my tongue or delay settling up with Hawkman over the little matter of my death.

The office door slammed open and the two beefcake thugs from earlier stood in its place. Behind them was Connor, who seemed to be Melli's right-hand man.

"Time's up," Connor announced. "Bobby's needed in training."

"What about me?" I asked, hand automatically going to a hip.

"What about you?" he asked back.

I wasn't used to being the one ignored, and it was a crappy, crappy feeling. At school, half the girls had wanted to be me, and the guys mostly wanted my digits. I flung my hair, but nearly dry it was no longer the weapon it had been. "I was in the middle of something anyway."

"Take her," Connor ordered.

But before they could, I stretched up to give Bobby a

kiss. His tongue darted between my lips, sending tingles all over, and then I was peeled away.

Thing One and Thing Two dragged me right back down to general population and tossed me in.

"Keep an eye on her," Thing One ordered the room at large. "Team Alpha, you're with us."

Half the room cleared out, pouring around me but not too close, like I might be contagious. Weirdly, they headed not toward the door but toward the back wall. The other kids cleared to the edges of the room, like someone had dripped soap into a greasy pot. I watched in disbelief as Things One and Two rapped out a little ditty on the floor, and the panel under their hands peeled back.

It looked like something out of *Tomb Raider* or *Indiana Jones*. I'd never suspected for even a second there was a trap door in here. It was totally cool. I made a note to pay more attention to the ditty next time, just in case the walls ever started closing in on me and I needed to make a quick getaway.

One by one, "Team Alpha" disappeared down the rabbit hole (Tina and Chaz thankfully among them), and I was left behind with a roomful of kids who were treating me like I had body odor or the plague or, like, terminally bad breath—Marcy among them. That was the one that twisted my gut.

There was no one for me to ask what the whole "Team Alpha" business was about. Maybe they were getting fed.

Maybe it was some kind of training, like Bobby was getting.

Whatever, Thing One's announcement had guaranteed that I'd be an outcast. I'd found some fragment of my old life, then lost it, all in one night.

10

An hour past sunset the next night I was ready to climb the walls. Everyone was avoiding looking at me, except when they thought *I* wasn't looking. I identified about ten seniors in all, including another of Chaz's wingmen (a forward or backward or whatever for the Mozulla Lemurs), Pam Raines and Vanessa Barrett (who had to have been taken together because I'd never seen them apart), Cassandra-the-cheerleader-Stiles (recovered from the hot-tubbing incident), and Trevor Larraby (an ROTC guy from his spit-shined shoes to his military bearing). There were probably twice that many underclassmen.

No one seemed inclined to talk as I passed by in my quest for a *Cosmo* or a *People* magazine that wasn't six months out of date. Not only had I totally skimmed all those issues already, but even if I wanted to go back and actually *read*, all the pictures of hotties, male and female, had been ripped out so that people could decorate the spaces around their cots. There wasn't a single story left intact.

I hadn't been assigned to either one of their stupid teams, so I couldn't get out for some exercise or just some fresh air—which would have been nice, because all those guys in one place trying to impress all those girls... well, you could practically smell the testosterone in the air. Only about half the time were the bathrooms used for their intended purpose. And they didn't *lock*. I'd already been scarred for life when I walked in on a couple of underclassmen playing topless tonsil hockey. There just wasn't enough mental floss to wipe out that image.

Whatever Melli was up to had to be big, for her to feed and house so many kids—a vamp army, as Rick had put it. If I didn't want to get left in the dust, I needed to gather some intel. I was pretty pleased with the super-spy sound of that, I must say. I could totally get into the glam international-woman-of-mystery wardrobe. I wondered if spy work came with a clothing allowance.

The first step in gathering intel had to be to get someone to talk to me. Marcy'd been avoiding me like I had the fashion flu, but I noticed a girl tucked away on a cot in the corner reading a book, completely oblivious to everything going on around her. She'd never see me coming. I stalked across the room like a lioness after prey. The girl didn't look up, even when my shadow fell across her book.

I reached down and plucked it away from her, at which she squeaked.

"Hi!" I said disarmingly.

Her eyes widened at the sight of me.

"Hi," she answered back, so tentatively it made me laugh.

"Hey, I don't bite ... well, I *do*. But then, so do you."

Her lips twisted in what might have been a smile. She had baby-fine blond hair held back by two kid barrettes with duckies on them, one pink and one purple. I tried not to stare.

"Can I have my book back?" she asked.

"In a sec," I agreed. "But I have a few questions first."

"Uh, okay."

I plunked myself down on the edge of her bed. "Why is everyone afraid of me?"

She looked at me in confusion. "Are they?" She glanced around, and half a dozen kids suddenly took extreme interest in the ceiling tiles. "Well, you did cause kind of a stir," she admitted.

"So?"

"So?" She looked longingly at her book, as if she might find the words she wanted within it. "Well, for some of us, getting vamped was the best thing that could have happened. I mean, sure, the biting bit was kind of a shock, and then the waking up dead … but aside from that."

I gave her the same look of horror I might give ruffles and spandex. "Ooh-kay. Let me get this straight—Melli sends her minions out to maul and murder and you're all grateful to her?"

The blond bookworm gave me a pitying look. "You make it sound so … ug. It's not like we're dead-dead. Anyway, you're not one of hers, so you can't possibly understand. She *chose* us."

"Each of you—personally?"

"We're all direct descendants. Her children, in a way. Some of us she saved from sucky situations at home or from lack of prospects after graduation."

"What about you?" I asked.

She looked away, and for a minute I thought she wouldn't answer. "You have no idea"—I was beginning to get a little steamed with her slights to my imagination— "what it's like to struggle for breath every day of your life and suddenly wake up to find it's no longer an issue."

"So you're … ?"

"Asthmatic. Severely. In and out of hospitals since I was a baby, two kinds of inhalers on me at all times. Nebulizer for emergencies. EpiPen. The whole nine yards. Now I'm cured."

"Now you're in prison," I said, looking around. "This place … it's like a barracks."

"I prefer to think of it as a dorm room," she answered. From the chill in her voice, I don't think I was making a new friend. "Anyway, it's temporary. She doesn't have any place else for us at the moment and she can't just have us all running around loose, causing mass hysteria, right?"

It made a sort of twisted sense, I supposed. And maybe the reason Melli kept Rick human and in school was to scout out the vulnerable kids, those easily cut out of the herd or with some reason to be thankful for their transformation.

"Can I have my book back now?" the girl asked. Then she added "*please*," like she'd only just remembered the magic word.

I couldn't think of any more questions at that moment. My mind was still reeling from her responses.

"Sure," I answered, glancing at the book before handing it back to her. *You Suck* by Christopher Moore. A vampire novel. Too funny.

Her smile was genuine this time, as she took the book and settled against the wall to read. I'd already ceased to exist for her.

So, smelly Melli commanded loyalty. There were probably as many reasons for that loyalty as there were kids, but I just couldn't see her as some kind of Lady Liberty, asking for our tired and poor, our huddled masses yearning to breathe free—although that's exactly what this girl was now doing.

I needed to learn more, and not just from someone

with a fairy-tale vision of the whole thing. I didn't trust Melli as far as I could throw her, especially with my new vamp strength.

And so I waited for the moment when I could slip my cage. I thought about doing it during the change of teams—when one returned and the other was called out— but it seemed there'd be too many people milling around then. Someone would be bound to notice. I could set up some kind of distraction for getting out, like jamming a hairpin or something into a socket and short-circuiting things, but with everyone's nifty new vamp-o-vision, I wasn't sure that would really do me any good. And I didn't see how it would help me slip back in unnoticed when my snooping was done … unless it somehow kicked up a real frenzy. But if that happened, chances were Melli's thugs would come running and do a little investigation, and I'd be snagged. I needed something low key, where everyone would be distracted …

Like Chaz and Tina putting on a really embarrassing show of PDA right there in the dorm, not even bothering with bathrooms and closed doors.

"Get a room!" someone called.

Someone else wolf-whistled.

Tina and Chaz didn't seem to notice. And no one seemed to notice *me* sliding off my boots so that I could slip silently into the hallway. There were no guards in the basement hallway, and the only sound was from the room

I'd just left behind, where I could now hear some guy taking bets on which base they'd hit.

I crept toward the stairs up to the main floor, the cinderblock cool on my stockinged feet, and listened again. Nothing. Either the coast was clear, or smelly Melli's guards were really quiet. I mean, she totally *had* guards, right? She couldn't just keep her thugs for kidnapping people and ripping off sporting goods stores, could she?

I poked my head out of the staircase and looked around. Still nothing. Well, I was no stranger to risk. It was the hallmark of high fashion. That and originality. Well, that and originality *and* the attitude to carry it off. I was all about attitude. I marched into that upstairs hallway like I had reason to be there, figuring it gave me more improvisational options if I was caught than if I was obviously sneaking. Perhaps I was just out looking for more fashionable footwear.

No one was there to care.

I walked toward Melli's office, waiting for someone to come by, but the Alpha and Beta teams had just switched places and evidently everyone was already where he or she was supposed to be. Except me. I pressed my ear up against Melli's office door.

"—the hell are you doing here?" I heard Mellisande hiss.

Okay, maybe not *just* me.

"You're not happy to see me? It is not a *special treat?*" There was something noxious about that voice. It wasn't all Crypt Keeper dark and spooky, but high and thin ... yet masculine, and completely lacking in anything resembling innocence. It was the kind of voice that led children away with candy, never to be seen again.

"Always," she was quick to insist. "But you ... here ... "

I see you, a voice said in my head, making me jump nearly out of my skin. The words seemed to beat against my brain like a thousand moths dashing themselves against a bright light.

At the same time the voice inside the room said, "But the *action* is here. All the pretty, pretty morsels under one roof. And the council ... ah, the council ... "

"What about them?" Melli asked, sounding impatient but afraid to quite show it. Interesting. "If you've told them anything—"

"You'll what? Kill me?" He laughed and it was madness, threatening to spread if it went on for too long. I was totally sure I'd be hearing it in my nightmares. "As I recall, you have already tried that."

"You came for a reason," Melli reminded him.

"Yes." He paused, and I imagined it was simply to make Melli crazy. I could almost like the guy for that. "But all you need to know is that the council is nearly at your door."

She was speechless for a moment. "Then I need to prepare." I heard curtains rustle, a window being lifted and thought that the first thing I'd do if I took over would be to soundproof my inner sanctum. "You'll see yourself out?" she asked.

"So...you'll be in my debt?" he asked slyly. It was no answer, but she didn't seem to realize it.

"I'll send your usual payment. Expect delivery tomorrow."

There was a smacking of lips that totally skeeved me out.

"Yes," he said, "I will."

I couldn't tell what happened next. There was a sound—maybe the guy jumping over the window sill—and then the click-click of Melli's spiked heels coming my way.

My heart nearly restarted in panic. I was sure the door to the office swung inward, which would give me no cover. Quickly I spun away and tried the next door, but it was locked and I was out of time.

Melli appeared in the hallway, and I waited for her to look my way and the ax to fall, but she never did. She walked so quickly toward the front of the house that I thought (okay, hoped) she'd break a heel.

I rushed to catch the office door before it closed, in case it was autolock, and nearly broke a nail doing it. I didn't have that many good ones left! Maybe Marcy'd have a home manicure kit or even just a file. Yeah, and maybe I could stab Thing One in the heart with it for turning her against me.

Come morsel. Here pretty pretty pretty. Just a little closer. I was already half inside the door when I froze, but it was not soon enough. Claws flashed out of nowhere and grabbed me by the shoulders. Next thing I knew, I was half off my feet and being dragged across the room, straight into the heavy gold curtains. It had all happened so fast. Unnaturally fast. The dust of the curtains made me choke and my eyes water, but that was the least of my worries. I looked up past the talons digging into my shoulders and into the face of the boogeyman. Bloodshot eyes stared into mine with the manic gleam of insanity, and the features were just ... wrong. He had all the right parts—two arms, two legs, nose, mouth, ears—all the appearance of humanity, and yet ... they were off, like the difference between jade and jadeite, all reconstructed and molded into a new form. Gave me the heebie jeebies.

And then he reached out with a black, pointed tongue to lick my nose.

"Ewww!" I cringed away from his rancid breath and the wet nastiness of the thing.

He smacked his lips and cocked his head as if considering what he'd tasted.

"Ahhh, the fly in the ointment."

My inner child was about to take me over and scream *Don't touch me* until someone big and strong came to kick his ass. But I didn't see that happening, so I locked her in a closet and mentally girded my loins or whatever.

"I'm not a fly."

He laughed and a swarm of spiders skittered up my spine. My skin seemed to tighten in an effort to get away. "More like the butterfly beating its wings that causes the monsoon halfway across the world."

I didn't get the whole butterfly thing, but it beat the hell out of being a common housefly.

"I'll tell you what I told *her*," he said, tasting me again, as if it were the cost of doing business. "The boy, morsel, *he matters*." Then his voice dropped to a near-normal octave and his eyes seemed to unfocus, like he was looking within. He murmured,

> *"The bonny boy debates*
> *The universe he holds in his hand.*
> *He is the key who will unlock the doors,*
> *The catalyst of change."*

Riddles. Oh joy. He couldn't have settled for knock-knock jokes ... or even limericks? "I don't get it," I said. "What boy? Bobby? What does it mean?"

"And *you*," he continued, as if I'd never spoken, "*You*, chick, chick, chick, are chaos made flesh. The boy is the key, but you will explode the locks."

While I was still processing that, he struck, yanking my head to the side to expose my neck. It felt as if a ring of needles pierced my flesh. Pain and terror made a toxic mix that turned my mind to mush. The violation of the bite froze me in horror and shot the toxic terror deep down inside, where I silently shrieked for it to stop. My sanity was hanging by a thread when the thing raised its mouth and I saw the needle-like teeth glistening with my blood. He licked them off, probably nicking his own tongue in the process, and the thought of the mingling of my blood and his nearly made me ill.

His eyes, which had rolled up into his head with pleasure, suddenly met mine and I felt pinned to a bug-board. "Stay. They come."

He released me and leapt like a creepy camel cricket for the open window, dragging it shut behind him just as the office door opened. I cringed back as far as I could go against the wall, hoping my feet and figure didn't show, hoping my neck wound had closed unnaturally fast and that I wouldn't be leaving a blood trail.

Most of all, though, I wanted that mental floss.

11

ight this way," Mellisande was saying, heels clacking on the floor as she approached. There were other footsteps as well, at least one set also in heels, but I didn't dare peek.

"We thank you for seeing us on ... no notice at all. The council has been hearing some disturbing things about you, Mellisande." The voice was much deeper than that of the boogeyman, but just as eerie. "They say that you're building an enclave with an eye toward empire. Might I remind you that your sire's death, which we have still not heard satisfactorily explained, released you only from his control, not *ours.*"

My opinion of the source of that voice went from bad to worse. He sounded smooth as maple syrup, and just as sticky. I'd seen girls fall prey to guys who sounded like that, implying insults without ever coming straight out with them, their extreme attention almost flattering at first. Then started the comments on appearance—the length of a skirt, the amount of makeup—and escalated into crazy jealousy and even violence. Totally obvious if you asked me, but power, even the wrong kind, had a way of attracting. The urge to look was nearly killing me; I liked to know my enemies, and I was pretty sure he'd be one of them.

"Please, sit," Mellisande responded. I wondered if she knew she sounded like royalty granting her subjects an audience. She seemed in control, completely recovered from her earlier shake-up with the mystery menace. "Let's discuss these outrageous accusations. I would like to know who has been making such claims, so that I can face my accuser."

A new voice spoke—feminine, lilting. "Then you deny the claims?"

"I do."

"Despite the fact that the mortality rate, particularly among teens, in your town has jumped since your return?"

Take that, Melli-noma, I thought.

"You blame *me* for the mortality rate among *children*? They are fearless, reckless with their own lives—"

"Malleable," the male voice chimed in again, and I thought it was pretty clear he didn't run in my circles if he thought we were all, like, totally suggestible. There'd be a lot fewer fashion disasters in this world if that were the case.

But if that's what Mellisande thought—that people would just pass off our deaths as due to reckless high spirits or something—then it made sense she'd be recruiting teens. And if she thought we were easily led ... well, okay, maybe the Tina Carstairs of the world were, but most of the kids I knew lived to piss off rather than please authority.

"Just so that I understand, what am I supposed to have done with these children?"

There was silence, as if the council clique thought the quiet would break her. Or—

"Franco, you know your mind tricks don't work on me," Melli scolded.

He laughed, but it was dry and false. "So I've heard, but here you are trying to convince me that these accusations are without merit. I thought it worth the attempt, to separate fact from fiction."

"How about you? Will you test me too?" Melli asked Franco's partner.

"I'd rather talk about the boy," the woman answered.

Melli asked, "What boy?" but it didn't come out as casually as she probably meant it to.

"Come now," the man barged in again. "We have our own pet psychic."

I thought about the totally creepy ... thing ... I'd come

face-to-face with behind these very curtains. There was no way he was domesticated. Maybe a pet in the sense that he'd be thrilled to bite the hand that feeds, but beyond that … I shuddered.

"I'm sure there are as many prophecies out there as there are prophets," Melli answered. "But it so happens that I have heard of a boy. I've been working to procure him for you, and plan to turn him over to the council to show my fealty."

My head was spinning. After the psychic's prophecy and the gemstone that lit up like a supernova around Bobby that first night, I was sure he must be "the boy." But Melli claimed to still be looking … She had to be lying. But then, why admit to knowing about him at all? Why reveal that secret, and yet keep others? My brain hurt. I had the desperate urge to burst into the room and demand answers, but the few brain cells that weren't tied up trying to make sense of the conversation held me back. The odds were against me. But if they actually tried to cart my boyfriend away, that would be a whole 'nother can of whup-ass.

"If you're harboring neither the boy nor your own piti-ful army, then you won't mind if we tour your facility," the man's slimy-sweet voice said.

A jolt of fear went through me—not that I cared if they delivered smelly Melli a smackdown over her lies, but what would that mean for my classmates? For Bobby? I mean, Melli wasn't exactly a laugh riot, but I didn't know that these guys were any better. Melli could make anyone snarky, so I didn't exactly hold that against them, but they seemed to have entire ten-foot poles stuck up their butts.

Melli responded with, "Not at all," still cool and unconcerned. Either she had some kind of crazy conceal-ment mojo I hadn't yet seen, or the boogeyman's warning had given her time to be sure all her toys were put away. I couldn't imagine where, but that was probably the point. "James and Roman will show you around. I will join you momentarily."

But-but-but, my brain stuttered, what if the council vamps used their "mind tricks" on those two? Wouldn't they spill the beans? I risked a peek out of the curtains, moving them just the tiniest fraction and almost buck-ling in relief to see that James and Roman were Things One and Two, the studs who'd pulled me out of general population the other night. They hadn't been in the room when the gemstone flared, and with luck they wouldn't know that Bobby was the boy they were supposed to be looking for. But they *did* know about Mellisande's teen army—unless the dragon lady had somehow been able to wipe their minds, in which case she was way tougher than I'd given her credit for. It freaked me out that right at this moment I was glad we were on the same side. But if she tried anything with Bobby—

I was still frozen behind the curtain, shut in with the dragon lady, when her office door opened and closed again. I could spy only a sliver of the room, a direct path to the door, but it was enough to see Connor slip in. And for him to totally catch my eye. He'd have to be blind not to see me peeking, and I could tell by the widening of his eyes that there wasn't the faintest hope of that. My whole body tensed, ready to spring into action, even if I didn't know what that action would be yet—jump out the window after the boogeyman, or fight my way to the door to warn Bobby that Melli-noma wanted him as some kind of pawn.

Then Connor did the unexpected. His gaze slid away, like there'd been nothing to see. "Teams Alpha and Beta are well away, playing the war game they call 'paintball,'" he reported in that delicious unplaceable accent of his. "Their facilities have been sanitized." I wondered what *that* meant. "Your new boy toy is likewise elsewhere."

"Very good. Once the council lackeys are gone and everyone is back, we'll dole out Rick's punishment. After kowtowing to the council, I feel the need for a good blood-letting."

Connor bowed and motioned for Melli to proceed him out of the room. But as soon as she was out, he shut the door behind her and turned on me.

A chill went straight up my spine as his eyes met mine.

"Front and center," he ordered.

I wondered if it was too late to jump out that window. But he hadn't ratted me out to the dragon lady, so maybe I should hear him out. Besides, if I wasn't going to jump, I was going to need to find allies somewhere. No one in the dorm was clamoring to be my new BFF.

I slid out from behind the curtain, feeling a little like I was facing the principal after cutting school, but detention wasn't the worst that could happen. Not with someone who'd reacted so casually to orders for a bloodletting.

"What?" I asked, trying to sound unconcerned, like I lurked behind curtains all the time and no one else had ever seemed to mind.

"You don't belong here," he said sternly.

"Well, since you've mastered the obvious, you totally don't need me. I'll just be on my way." It wasn't the thing to say if I was looking for friends, but it just slipped out. And anyway, if he was going to respect anything it wouldn't be fear.

"No," he answered firmly. "You won't."

I stared straight into those wicked green eyes of his and threw my shoulders back, but his eye wasn't as easily drawn as Rick's had been. "Look, if you were going to sound an alarm, you would have done it. So, chances are you're operating outside the system here, which means you don't want me kicking up a fuss." He narrowed his eyes at me. "In which case you should probably just get to your point and not try anything funny."

He laughed, a short bark of humor. "You're so like her. Both of you scrapping at the world with no idea what you're up against."

"Wow, you sure know the way to a girl's heart." Had that accent really made me gooey that first day? Go figure.

"You're missing one thing," he continued, matching

my sidestep as I tried to sidle around him. "What I know about *you* would get you killed. And I will expose it, *expose you*, to save myself. Unless you help me."

That stumped me. "What do you know about me?"

I could practically see the wheels turning in his head as he tried to decide what would get him further, buying my goodwill with the info or stringing me along. I crossed my arms.

"Spill," I ordered.

He sighed. "You've inherited one of Mellisande's very rare powers. For some reason it seems to have skipped a generation. I've been watching, but none of her direct descendants have her resistance to mesmerism. I tried it on you that first day, and you shook me off." Well, *that* explained the hot toddies. "Mellisande only knows that she can't effortlessly reach you the way she can her children. She has not yet dug deeper. Once she learns she can't control you, you're of no use to her. She doesn't trust anyone she can't control."

"Like she controls you?"

His face contorted, and I could tell he was pissed that I'd put my finger on it. "Like she controls me," he growled. "When she focuses. Luckily, our lady has a lot on her plate just now."

"So, how does my power"—and sure, I couldn't get a cool one like invisibility or mind-reading or anything— "help you?"

"I'm still working on that. When the time comes, I

will let you know. For now, we can start with what you've overheard."

"What, you don't have the place wired?" I asked.

"Mellisande does sweeps against listening devices," he explained. "Any I set would be discovered."

If she was that paranoid, she probably left her office door unguarded so the guards couldn't eavesdrop, figuring no one would be stupid...er, brave...enough to stand in an exposed hallway and listen in. Little did she know.

This felt like a moment of truth. If Connor was testing me on Melli's orders to see if I could be trusted with her secrets, I would fail the moment I opened my mouth. If, on the other hand, he truly was in this for himself and thinking of staging some kind of coupe—no, wait, a coupe was a car, right?—well, anyway, some kind of power grab, then he was going to crush me if I didn't climb on board.

I thought about those resentful looks he'd thrown at the dragon lady when she wasn't looking. I was pretty sure he wasn't playing me out of loyalty to *her*, but would throwing my lot in with him be any better than cozying up to Melli? I mean, trying to control me at first sight with thoughts of grody bearskin rugs didn't exactly give him a gold star in my little black book. Maybe I could set myself up as some kind of double agent, at least until I could figure out what was what.

I shrugged. "Okay, then. What I overheard—*CliffsNotes* version: the council is on to Melli. They suspect she's been collecting kids and, for some reason, they want Bobby."

"Why?"

"I was kind of hoping you'd tell me. That glowy gemstone thing—"

"Medallion," he corrected. "It glows in the presence of power. Our undead state may come with parlor tricks like mesmerism and the like, but you'd be surprised how little *true* power goes along with that. Magic is rare. Magic is power. I'm not surprised Mellisande sought Bobby out, if someone pointed her in his direction."

"But—"

"Shh!" he hissed. Footsteps approached, and I wondered if I was going to have to hustle again for those curtains, but the steps kept right on going. I wasn't about to spill about Bobby being "the key" and all that, in case Connor decided the way to one-up Melli would be to turn Bobby over to the council himself. This way, maybe he'd spend more time trying to figure out how he could use Bobby closer to home, like he was planning to use me. I just hoped he didn't view Bobby as a rival for the power he clearly wanted for himself.

"You should go now," Connor said, once the footsteps had faded away. "I've got arrangements to make."

"But—"

"*Now*," he said, and I felt a vague wash of sensation sweep over me, like all the hair on my body had been ruffled at once ... like he'd been trying to influence me, even though he knew it wouldn't work.

"Whatever," I said back. Wasn't like I was getting answers anyway. At least I was starting to figure out the questions.

I crept back through the hallways, no thanks to my new co-conspirator, who went his own way instead of providing me cover. Luckily, the halls were still eerily deserted. It was like a ghost town.

When I got to the dorm, I saw that "sanitized" meant that all the pictures had been taken off the walls and the beds stacked up like they weren't in use. Product had been cleared from the bathrooms, which made them seem almost spacious. I'd seen spy shows where cleaners could make a whole crime scene disappear, but I'd never have believed it could be done so quickly if I hadn't witnessed it. Melli had even gone so far as to have her people use an unscented cleanser. With my vamp senses I could smell it if I inhaled deeply, but it wasn't the tell-tale pine or lemon I was used to at home, or even the really industrial chemical scent of the one they splashed all over school.

I hated to hand it to the lady, but maybe she wasn't just a pretty face. Dammit.

12

My classmates returned, erupting up through the trap door and pouring into the room, only to crash up against each other like the Three Stooges when they saw the complete desolation of their space. It was clear that no one had warned them, and they all looked at me—the single near-living thing in the room, sitting on the solitary bunk I'd pulled down for myself—in accusation.

"Not me," I said in defense, but no one could really hear me over the indignant cries of the kids who couldn't make it out of the hole because those who had stopped cold were jamming up the works.

Things One and Two were no help. They pushed through, ignoring questions with a simple, "We'll be back." Luckily, they returned before the tide could really turn on me, with two Santa-sized bags of belongings, toiletries, and sundries. The place erupted into chaos. It looked like the year-end sale at Bergdorf's—kids fighting over this picture or that shirt, neither of which made out well in the melee.

I watched with a kind of reality-show fascination until something moved in to block my view.

I looked up to see that Marcy had planted herself in front of me, fists jammed into her hips, and I thought, *here we go.*

"Do you believe this?" she asked, and I looked around to see which *this* we were talking about—because I could well believe anything at this point.

But she wasn't looking at the mayhem all around us, only at the globs of bright purple paint decorating her outfit like so-called modern "art."

"Um," I began cautiously.

She flopped down next to me on the bed and I hoped she'd had time to dry, but I didn't think so. "Not that I dressed up or anything. I mean, they *warned* us when they called us all out for their little war games, but still. This is never coming out."

I blinked. "I thought you weren't talking to me."

She gave me a pout she'd stolen from my arsenal. "Oh,

come on, like anyone else feels my pain. This tank is *raw silk*. Besides, I can't stay mad at you. You're the only one here who knows a Jimmy Choo from a Margaret Cho."

"Isn't she a comic?" I asked.

"See!" she answered triumphantly, bumping my shoulder companionably.

I bumped her back, even if I was still a little steamed.

"So, why aren't you in the melee?" I asked.

She rolled her eyes to the ceiling. "Please! Like this stupid game"—she flicked a hand at her purple splotches—"didn't wreak enough havoc on my manicure. And whoever wins is just going to get their picture grabbed the second their back is turned. Not really worth the effort. Besides, have you seen the eye candy around here? Two dimensional boyfriends are kind of ... lame, you know?"

Now we were speaking my language. "So, who do you have your eye on?"

Marcy was just about to tell me when the doors to the hall burst open ... only this time it had nothing to do with me. For a whole entire second I'd forgotten about Melli and her plots and almost felt normal again. But if life was like a box of chocolates, then I was doomed to get the nasty maple filling.

Rick fell at our feet, pushed there by two of Melli's minions: Chickzilla and Hawkman. I glared daggers at them, but if they noticed they didn't give a damn, and only moved farther into the room so the rest of the dragon lady's entourage could enter—including Bobby. Not even thinking, I hurled myself at him and he caught me, his face grim and his gaze looking past me at Rick. I thought about what Melli had told Connor—about a bloodletting—and I turned as well.

Rick lay on the ground at Mellisande's feet, curled around his stomach like the bizarro-world demonstration of crime and punishment had already begun. He wore a sweat-stained tank top and shorts, as if he'd just come from a workout...or work-over, more like. My nose tingled at the smell. My lips twitched back in distaste, in horror, but still my eye-teeth grew. I could practically smell his fear, like a tang in the air. Within me, something elemental that I wanted no part of responded.

I squeezed Bobby's hands until he said, "Ow! Gina, you're hurting me."

"But not as badly as they're going to hurt *him*, right?"

I didn't like Rick, and I had hurt him myself, but *this* was different. It was, like, ganging up. And with some of the gangees vamps and him just a muscle-head, it didn't really seem fair. 'Course, as my parents were really fond of telling me, life wasn't fair. And death wasn't exactly going to pick up the slack.

Bobby looked remote, maybe struggling with his own inner nasty. I hoped so, anyway. I didn't want to think he was unaffected. "Looks like."

"Are you going to do anything?" I whispered.

"Like what?" Bobby's gaze kinda slid down to mine

for a second, less remote now but more hard, determined. "Gina, he *attacked* you!"

I tossed my hair. "He *tried*."

But Melli's enforcers were calling the lynch mob to order and there was no more time for talk.

Melli took the floor, drawing all eyes to her in her raspberry wraparound dress, her ankles wrapped with laces that crisscrossed down to matching heels. She looked like she'd just stepped off a runway, right over the cold dead bodies of her rivals.

"Rick disobeyed a direct order to leave a prisoner to rot," Melli began, pitching her voice to carry and looking straight at me. As a result, thirty-odd pairs of eyes turned on me with varying levels of confusion and anger, like it had been *my* fault Rick got all enterprising. I was used to being the center of attention, but not quite this way. As alternatives to the dragon lady, Connor and even the council were looking better and better. "His disobedience allowed the prisoner to escape, albeit not for long..." *Albeit*, who said that? "I think it's time you all learn the cost."

She raised a hand and her inner cabal—Connor, Larry, the beefcakes, a slim blond woman I hadn't seen before—fell on Rick like a ton of bricks.

Thing Two, the professor, bit into Rick's inner arm, spilling a drop that slid down his chin to drip on a scuffed shoe. Connor's eyes flashed before he sank *his* teeth into Rick's thigh. There was some artery there or something that I didn't think you could live without. Melli herself took his throat. I cried out, and Bobby squeezed my hand hard enough to grind the bones together. As with a train wreck, it was impossible to look away.

Rick convulsed when the first fangs hit. Then his lids lowered, as if too heavy, and his body relaxed slowly into what I hoped was sleep. The professor shifted and a sudden spurt of blood caught me right across the chest.

My eye teeth were now fully extended and Bobby whimpered beside me, but neither of us moved, paralyzed by the opposing pulls of horror and need. I didn't know which way I would have gone, but suddenly it was over. Connor raised his head and declared, "Enough. Don't follow him into death."

The vamp cabal's heads raised and they backed away, Mellisande last of all, eyes flashing at Connor's orders. Rick was left there, a rag doll fallen bonelessly to the floor. If he was still breathing, as Connor's words implied, I couldn't see it, and it didn't seem likely to continue for long. Bobby turned me toward his chest, as if to shelter me *now* from what was going on.

"Take him away," Melli ordered someone, but all I could see was Bobby's blue sweater.

"Everyone else, back to work," she ordered.

As if nothing momentous had taken place, the vamp cabal retreated, turning their backs on Rick and his fate and leaving the human minions—Chickzilla, Sparky, and Hawkman—to dispose of his remains. The rest of us stood in stunned silence.

No one had intervened. *No one.* Not even me.

I'd become one of the monsters.

I wanted to hit something, and Bobby was my closest target. I pummeled at his sides, at his chest, but he only gripped me tighter. Then, through a haze of anger, I realized that he was pulling me somewhere out into the hallway, and the fight just went out of me. I pushed him away, blinking through the red haze at the stain I'd left on his nice sweater. I'd wept blood. Well, if that didn't say it all.

Bobby'd only let me push him so far—to the end of his reach. His hands still gripped my shoulders.

"Gina," he said gently, "there was nothing we could do. We have to pick our battles."

Even as softly as he'd spoken, I knew how sound bounced around in this place and nodded toward a door farther down the corridor, the one that led to my short-term prison. He slid his hands down my arms until his left hand gripped my right and led me in the direction I'd indicated. Both the outer and inner doors to my cell area were mercifully unlocked, now that no one was occupying them.

I yanked my hand out of his, my eyes blazing. "So, picking our battles means we let people die?"

"He's not dead … yet," Bobby hedged. "And I didn't see you—"

"Don't! Just don't, okay?" I suddenly wasn't feeling so hot, as if the bloodlust had blazed through me like a wildfire, leaving nothing but its hunger behind. "First there's your crazy dam, then the psychic, the council, Connor's coupe ... what's next?"

I collapsed into the single guard chair and put my head in my scaly hands. "*Plus,* if I don't get some moisturizer and a nail file in the next twenty-four hours, I think I'm going to scream."

Bobby looked ... amused ... and that was just so wrong I didn't have words.

"Well, at least you've got your priorities. And you're going too fast for me. What's all this about a psychic and a car?"

I groaned. "I don't mean a coupe, do I? Like a 'coo' or whatever, when someone wants to take over. Far as I can tell, your sugar momma is playing a power game with some kind of vampire council. This creepy psychic guy I saw says that you're 'the key' and I'm, like, 'chaos.' And then, Connor's trying to blackmail me ... "

Bobby's head looked about ready to spin. "You lost me at 'coo.' Wanna start at the beginning?"

I huffed, but I did the best I could, starting with sneaking out of the dorm.

He blew out a breath. "You *have* been busy."

"What has the dragon lady had you doing? Not just cooling your heels, I'll bet."

"I'm learning to use my powers. And, Gina, it's totally cool. They're not saying so, 'cause I don't think they want me to know their limitations, but I don't think what I do is totally normal."

He looked like the geek-boy who'd just been given the keys to the comic shop.

"I think you're right. So, what can you do?"

His incredible blue eyes lit with excitement. "I can move stuff around, move *people* around—or convince them to move, anyway, like some Jedi mind trick. And not just one at a time. " He squatted so his eyes were level with mine and reached out to touch my face. "I'm still learning, but I can do it well enough to protect us and get us out ... soon ... because whatever's going on around here sounds like trouble."

"Not without Marcy," I said.

"And everybody else," he agreed. "Which is why we can't be all impulsive. If we want to free everyone and stop whatever Mellisande's cooking up, it's going to take time. And a plan."

That made sense, but I still didn't like it. Patience just seemed like such a waste of time. There were more of us than there were of smelly Melli and her cabal, and maybe after what they'd seen with Rick they'd be fired up to escape ... or maybe they'd be scared spitless and someone would tattle to the dragon lady, ruining our chances. No, Bobby was right, darn it. I had to learn the *P* word.

"Fine," I said, maybe not as graciously as I could have. "What have you learned so far? I get that we're comatose with the dawn, but do we really burn up in sunlight? What about stakes and crosses and holy water and ... "

"Whoa, slow down." He got that totally hot glint in

his eyes, like I'd done something sexy just spouting off at the mouth. "I had no idea you were into vamp lore."

I rolled my eyes. "Please. I wouldn't know a thing if Hollywood didn't make the vampires so smokin'."

"You think vampires are smokin'?" he asked.

"Well, one in particular."

His eyes were totally smoldering now and he licked his lips, but he didn't let that divert him. "Well, crosses, holy water, stars of David and all that won't do anything unless they're blessed or have real faith behind them. They don't work if they're just decoration. I'm trying not to think about what that means for our souls. Larry said even going past an Italian place now makes him choke, so I'm guessing garlic works. But I think the whole thing about vampires not being able to cross running water is just to lull prey—"

"Bobby," I cut in.

"Yeah?"

"Shut up and kiss me."

Somewhere during his speech I'd decided I was way more interested in him than what he was saying. He took a step closer and I slid my hands beneath his sweater, wanting to feel his skin, the tautness of his muscles. I stroked my nails down his back and he gasped and bent his head down to kiss me.

All thoughts of mortality and escape fled my brain.

13

I was still waiting my turn in line for one of the bathrooms, rubbing sleep out of my eyes—the sandman still came, even if the dreams didn't—when the dormitory doors opened. Dread rose up in me. It totally reinforced the fact that something had to be done. I was not going to live my life in fear of an opening door.

Sparky and Chickzilla stood there, scanning the crowd.

"Marcy Soleas," Chick said, raising her voice so that it bounced ominously around the room.

Marcy, who was right in front of me in line doing her

standing stomach exercises while she waited (even though I was pretty sure blood was a low-carb diet and that the transformation would let her keep her abs of steel), whirled around at the sound of her name, took in Melli's minions and got a death grip on my arm.

All eyes turned toward Marcy. Chickzilla and Sparky followed their lead.

"Come with us," Chick continued. She tried to make her voice neutral, maybe even upbeat, but she failed.

Marcy's nails were like talons digging into my arm. "I *knew* it. I suck at the war games. I'm, like, the worst of the worst. *I'm next.*"

I didn't want to believe it, but being singled out by this gang hadn't exactly been good for Rick ... or me. So not comforting. Around us everyone watched with wide-eyed attention. Pam Raines and Vanessa Barrett even stopped their incessant whispering. Chaz and one of his wingmen looked like they might almost consider stepping up if there was undisputed proof that Marcy was in danger ... or if there was something in it for them. It seemed that the attack on Rick had scratched everyone's rose-colored glasses.

"Why?" I challenged the Chick.

"Because the lady said so," Sparky answered for her.

"I want to go too." A hand went to my hip as I said it, and I heard Chaz take a breath as if he recognized the danger sign.

"No. There, that was easy. *Marcy*," Sparky said, like maybe his summons carried more weight than the Chick's.

Marcy took a step forward, still with the death grip on my arm, which pulled me out of line. I gave her hand a squeeze, then gently pried her nails from my flesh.

"Nothing's going to happen. Promise," I told her.

"Pinky swear?" she whispered back.

"Absolutely."

Chickzilla rolled her eyes skyward. "Lord, pinky swear? Where are we, grade school?"

I turned on her. "Speaking of which, the '80s called. They want their clothing back." Her outfit today was a baby blue unitard with a silver sheen. She looked like she belonged in some ancient video where the men wore more makeup than the women.

She actually grinned. "Nice face. Get it out of a Crackerjack box?"

"All right," Sparky snarled. "We're on a time table, so if you two are done with your hissy fit…"

The Chick glared at him and started across the room to grab Marcy, since she wasn't moving quickly enough on her own. They marched her out into the hall, the door swinging shut behind them.

No way in hell was I letting anyone I cared about end up like Rick. I had a sudden really deep suspicion about where they were taking Marcy and why, and I had a feeling she wouldn't be coming back. I was going to get my boots on and then I was going to kick some ass.

I looked around my cot. "Who the *hell* has my boots?" I asked, glaring straight at Tina. "If none of you have the cojones to follow them, surrender my spikes and get out of my way."

The boots flew across the room to land at my feet—hurled by, of all people, Chaz, who must have swiped them for Tina, because the alternative, some kind of fetish, was just too freaky to think about.

"Hair spray," I added.

"Gina, now isn't the time—" Tina started, and I growled.

No one else even asked. A can of superhold flew out of nowhere and I caught it one-handed. Pretty cool. I tucked it into my waistband like a pistol. Not quite pepper spray, but it would do.

"Now, where's that trap door?" I was already cursing myself for not paying better attention.

Cassandra, the cheerleader, blew out a breath so strong it lifted her blond hair right off her face. "*I'll* show you." She glared around the room. "Any of you say a word, you're dead meat. Get me?"

A few people nodded, but mostly no one moved at all.

"This way," she continued.

I followed her to the very area where all the beds were stacked. She turned again to the room at large. "A little help here?"

This much they could do. The room unfroze; kids came to unstack their beds, move them away until the space was cleared. It was a good job. If I didn't know there was a door, I'd never have seen it. For the first time, I wondered if Melli had had it installed or if it had started as some old bomb shelter or something—not that Ohio was, like, a hotbed of strategic targets.

"Anyone know the code?" I asked.

"That's the trick, isn't it?" ROTC-guy, Trevor, asked, stepping forward. "It's a little complicated; it takes two." He looked at Cassandra, who blushed.

I felt distinctly like a third wheel.

"But I don't know it," she admitted.

Looking into her eyes, he took her hand and then played a beat on her palm with his other hand. "It's like dum de-adda, dum de-adda, dum de-adda, dum de-adda."

"'Chopsticks'?" I asked incredulously, but also quietly, because I didn't want to be a buzzkill when they were helping me out. His part would then have to be "Heart and Soul," the first thing any kid learned to play on the piano … even me, though the piano teacher my parents foisted on me and I mutually agreed to part ways before someone got hurt.

Cassandra nodded to Trevor that she had it, and they squatted next to the slab to play their duet. The trap door recessed into the floor and slid back.

I sat down on the edge of the opening to slide my boots on, because if I were jumping into the unknown I didn't want it to squish between my toes. Something in the toe of one boot went crinkle-crunch. It beat ooze or squish, but not when my brain suggested bugs, or their carcasses, that could have taken up residence while I was away. I tried to tell myself it was just someone's Corbin Bleu picture or something, and that time was awastin'. I knew Marcy was getting farther and farther away—and that was enough of a motivation to make me jump down into that hole.

Because if I was right, Marcy was Melli's "payment" to creepy psychic guy.

He seemed like the type who enjoyed playing with his food, which should at least give me some time. I only hoped Marcy could stick it out, and that I'd come up with some kind of plan between here and there—once I figured out where "there" was.

"Wish me luck," I said to Cassandra and Trevor.

I was surprised to hear more than two voices come back to me. It made my heart swell as I pushed off from the edge and landed hard below.

"You know, there's a ladder," Trevor called down … too late.

"Yeah, thanks," I answered wryly.

I straightened up, trusting the super vamp healing to take care of the pain in my knee.

"Got a flashlight?" I asked. But nobody did, and I was on my own in the near-total dark. Once that trap door closed above me, it would be like a solar eclipse. Good thing I'd never been scared of the dark, just the creatures that skittered around in it.

I tried to focus on a plan and not thoughts of mice or

cockroaches or millipedes. Definitely not millipedes. All those legs...I shuddered.

Several steps into the tunnel, something brushed my shoulder and I yipped before realizing it was just a string dangling from a light fixture in the ceiling. I pulled, and above me the trap door started to close. They'd waited until I had light. If I passed by a Starbucks on my way back from rescuing Marcy, the lattes were on me.

Meanwhile, I blinked against the sudden light. I was in a bunker-type area, all industrial shelves stocked with enough stuff to weather an apocalypse—if I was still baseline human, that is. I wondered how well blood would keep and whether Melli planned to stock her own donors if she was ever forced down here. But the tunnel continued on past this room, and I didn't have time to explore. I jogged into the tunnel, hoping there was another light in it somewhere.

My knee wasn't recovering as quickly as it should, and very nearly buckled a few strides in, which was freakish. But not as worrying as the wave of dizziness that followed. Now that I thought about it, I hadn't eaten in days—not since I'd first risen. People, I thought, could go three days without food. Was it better or worse for vamps?

Through sheer force of will I put on a burst of speed, running flat-out in spiky-heeled boots not meant for it, until I reached the end of the tunnel. I didn't have anyone to help me with the musical code here, so I just had to hope that it was (a) the same at this end and (b) acceptable for me to do one part with each hand.

It took me a few tries, because the left hand kept wanting to do what the right hand was doing, but I finally got it and the door above slid open, showering me with a fine spray of dirt. I emerged in the woods, but a streetlight off to my right was like a beacon back to civilization. I ran toward it—and was startled to break into the school parking lot, near the gym and athletic fields. I was even more startled to see a car there waiting for me, and the door pop open at my approach.

And inside ... Rick ... looking halfway to dead, but still Rick. For the second time in an hour my heart felt like someone had goosed it with, like, a thousand volts and it might as well just explode as restart.

Rick was *alive*. Sort of, anyway. I mean, he looked terrible: circles under the eyes, a grayish complexion, gaunt like he'd lost mass overnight, and just barely keeping himself upright by hanging onto the steering wheel of a cream-colored T-bird, a far cry from Bobby's POS.

"Rick!" I said stupidly.

"Get in!" he answered.

I just stared. "But what ... how?"

He rolled his eyes to the sky. "Didn't you get the note?"

Note? Right, the crunchy thing in my boot, maybe. "Uh, no."

"Whatever. Come on. Connor said to grab you."

That, at least, made sense. Connor could have faked

Rick's death and set Rick up as his eyes on the outside. But how had he known I'd be here? Unless his note instructed me to do exactly what I was doing anyway, which had an eerie kind of inevitability to it, like the bottom falling out of the Beanie Baby market.

I shivered like someone had walked over my grave, but I got in the car. What else was I going to do? Someone had to save Marcy.

Rick peeled out before my door was even fully closed, which was when I realized I was taking for granted that we were thinking along the same lines.

"Off to save Marcy, right?" I asked.

"Who? Whatever. I'm just here to play chauffeur."

I hoped the note in my boot was more enlightening. I reached down to unzip and Rick said, "Oh, by all means, make yourself comfortable."

"You wish," I sneered, shaking out the crumpled paper that had molded to my big toe. "This is all that's coming off."

"Pity."

My nose kind of crinkled with *ick* as I unfolded the note.

Get to the high school. Someone will meet you there.
You want to save your friend; I want to know about
the prophecy. Come back with the information or not
at all.

Short, sweet, and to the point ... only without the sweet. It didn't actually say that Rick would be the "someone" or that I should suddenly trust him as far as I could throw him, only that I would be provided with the means to find the psychic and grill him about the prophecy. Of course, I'd failed to mention to Connor that I more or less knew the prophecy already. And Connor had failed to care about Marcy, beyond using her rescue as incentive.

"Let me ask you, why does Connor need me to run his little errand?" I asked Rick, watching him closely. "Why doesn't he make you do it?"

Rick shot me a venomous look. "You don't know much, do you? From what I hear, the psychic doesn't like my kind."

"Male?"

"Breathing."

"Oh." I thought about that. Could be that if the psychic did like to play with his food, humans just weren't sporting. Too quick to die.

Not a happy thought.

"You haven't told me where we're going," I said finally.

"Don't know exactly." And yet he was twisting and turning down back roads like he had some clue, still draped over the steering wheel for support. "Connor said you'd know."

"Oh yeah—?" *Morsel*, a voice whispered through my head; it felt like spiders on creepy, prickly little legs, like an invasion. *Come, morsel. Come, pretty pretty pretty. Two for one. And all for me. What a treat.*

"You do know you guys are being watched, right?"

Rick continued, as if he hadn't heard anything at all. No spiders were skittering through his head.

"Excuse me?" I managed to ask, distracted.

"Someone," he said, like I was a dimwit. "Watching Melli's place. Council, I figure. Might want to let Connor know."

Here, morsel, the voice in my head continued to whisper, blowing tendrils of inky, multi-legged invasion through my brain.

My lips curled. "Ew, ew, ew!" Everything in me shrieked that we should turn and run, put the pedal to the metal. "We're supposed to go *toward* that?"

"Toward what?"

"That," I answered, wanting to beat at my own head to stop the psychic infestation, which was still skittering through my brain. The whispers seemed to slip into all the dark pathways, opening the Pandora's box of fears I locked away.

"Turn," I said through gritted teeth.

"Which way?"

Back, I wanted to tell him. "Left," I said instead.

Rick took the next left, into an abandoned industrial site blocked off by an iron gate gone to rust. The headlights swept it, and with a "Holy crap" Rick stopped short. "This is as far as I go," he said.

I was guessing the place had finally gotten to him as well. Maybe he was getting some hint of the whispers that were now so loud, so overlapping, they nearly drowned out the sound of his voice.

Against my will, my hand reached for the door handle and I stumbled onto the cracked drive before I could stop myself. Whatever this thing was, I couldn't just shake it off like I had Connor's little compulsion. It was more primal and powerful than that. Than me.

If I lived through this, Connor was dead meat. "You'll wait!" I called back to Rick.

"For a while," he agreed—sort of.

It was going to have to be enough, because my feet were already carrying me onward. I couldn't help but wonder why Connor didn't just grill the boogeyman himself if it was so important to him. Maybe he was afraid Melli would notice his absence, though I'd bet he just didn't want to get within spitting distance of the psycho-psychic.

I discovered that if I fought the compulsion *really* hard, I could stop myself from skirting around that gate, from going farther up the walk toward the building that was a mere blocky shape in the distance... if I wanted to shake, sweat, and generally jitter like a junky. But I was a ma'am on a mission, and I would go on. The T-bird's headlights illuminated my path to hell—which, contrary to popular belief, was completely unpaved.

Between lack of food and the free-for-all going on in my head, I was really shaky by the time I neared the building, which looked like it should probably be condemned. *Come on, bit bit bit. Come, morsel.* I'd never been so creeped out in all my life, not even when Larissa'd had that Halloween slumber party where we watched the *Nightmare on Elm Street* marathon and her boyfriend jumped out at us in a Freddy Krueger mask.

"Get the hell out of my head!" I screamed, mentally and physically. Maybe I had some vain hope that our psychic connection ran both ways and I could somehow make him recoil, but mostly I just couldn't take it any more. I wanted to drown out the whispers, if only for a second.

Hysterical laughter filled my head. *The mind of a teen-aged girl is indeed a terrifying thing.*

Steam didn't actually come out of my ears, but it was a very near thing. I was eager now for the showdown, and the anticipation propelled me the last few feet toward the warped warehouse door. It stood ajar, like nothing within the building had anything to fear from without. Boarded-up windows gave no clue of what beckoned.

The knob I reached for had been painted in the same flaking black as the door itself. Even with the compulsion on me, it looked totally too grody to touch. I grasped at the bottom of my cami—the thing was destined for the incinerator at this point anyway—and used it to pull the door toward me. It groaned at the movement, paint flecking off the whole way.

Inside it was pitch dark, except for the light I was letting in from outside and a weird glow off to the right. My eyes adjusted in, like, no time flat, but they needn't have bothered. There was nothing to see here unless abandoned warehouses buttered your bread. Personally, debris, cobwebs, a lifetime supply of dust, and creepy things scurrying along the floor didn't do it for me. And the *smell*. If I actually had to breathe, I'd probably choke on the air, which was thick and heavy with the scent of voided bowels and spoiling meat, blood, and mold.

"Anyone here?" I called—but, you know, not *too* loudly.

Come, morsel, the voice said, giving me the jitters. *Toward the light, the better to see you, my dear.*

It's your freak show, I responded mentally.

The whispering in my head quieted all of the sudden as if listening, then answered, "Out of the mouths of babes."

Only *this* time the voice wasn't in my head—and that didn't make it any better. It was again that high-pitched croon. I bet he drove the neighborhood dogs to distraction.

I followed the sound, into a dark room lit only by a lantern in the center. I kicked something and it rolled before me ... sounded like bone, not that I was any expert. I tried not to look, but it was instinctual ... and it was a bone. Femur, maybe, or some other long bone. Big enough to be ... my brain balked. The bone rattled into others like it, the remains of several meals at least. And there, cowering in the corner, was Marcy.

"You okay?" I asked.

"Y-y-yes," she answered unconvincingly.

"Great. *Run!*"

She cut her gaze toward the boogeyman and then bolted for the doorway. I stepped aside to let her through, but in one quick leap, more worthy of a grasshopper than anything human-shaped, the psychic cut her off.

Marcy screamed as he grabbed her shoulders and thrust her back, into a pile of bones, like she was a mere rag doll. I stooped to pick up a weapon, not that I thought it would do me any good against him. It didn't make me feel much more powerful than my blazing fury alone.

"Trade," I said, hefting the—I looked down—skull. It was all I could do not to scream. "Her for me."

He looked at me in amusement, eyes blazing red now like Melli's never had, and that crazy laughter bounced around in my brain. "Why, when I could have you both?"

"Over my dead body."

"Eventually," he agreed.

I launched the skull at him, aiming it like a dodgeball at my arch-nemesis. Tina had just lost her title. She'd be sooo crushed.

The skull bounced off his chest. His eyes flared, but that was the only reaction. Not a flinch, not so much as a wince.

"I may cease to find you amusing," he threatened.

"That's a shame, 'cause I live for your amusement … Oh wait, I *don't*."

"Gina?" Marcy's voice quavered, but this time I ignored her, not wanting to switch my attention and possibly the freakshow's toward my friend.

"Gina!" she said more urgently, the edge of hysteria

creeping into her voice. I realized that the floor was moving...skittering...at the edges of my vision. Mice. Plural. Marcy would be freaking and scaling the walls any time now. Which I could handle, but her shrieking...Maybe the freakshow would have over-sensitive ears.

I couldn't count on that, though.

"Yo, dude, catch!" And I launched myself at him, yanking the hair spray from my waistband as I went. I did a duck and roll as his talons swept at me, grabbing up the lantern as I rolled past. The candle inside flickered and sloshed hot wax but didn't go out, and I used my momentum to hurl the lantern at the creep as hard as I could, unleashing a stream of superhold as the lantern flew by. The very air caught fire.

"Run, Marcy, *now!*" I yelled, hoping I'd foiled the creep's night vision, hoping that this was enough of a distraction. The flames didn't last long, though, and as he fought his way through them, Marcy shot past me to the door. Freakshow lurched, and I shot the hair spray again, right into his blazing red eyes.

His howl split my head in two. I dove for the door while he thrashed blindly, trying to grab me up or rip me to shreds. Either way, I wasn't waiting around to find out.

Rend, tear, taste, shred, kill. The thoughts burst in my head like a blood vessel. The boogeyman had murder in his heart, and I had been marked for death.

I *ran*. The death of the flames meant momentary blindness while my eyes readjusted, and I tripped and stumbled over things that rolled beneath my feet. Something nipped at my heels, feeling like the hounds of hell, though it was probably only the mice, spurring me on.

I burst out into the night, suddenly able to see, and raced for Rick and the car. Marcy was nowhere in sight.

"Marcy!" I yelled as I ran, but there was no answer. It was like the night had swallowed her whole.

She hadn't waited around, and I couldn't afford to either. That thing wouldn't be too far behind. At least she was alive. That was enough for now.

14

I slammed myself into the car and shut the door behind me yelling, "Go, go, go!"

Rick looked at me, startled, but was already shifting into reverse before the words were fully out of my mouth.

"Your friend?" he asked.

"Got away," I said, sucking in a quick breath to speak.

"The prophecy?"

"Got it," was my answer. No need to give him the time stamp on my information, which of course dated back to me hiding behind the curtains in Melli's office.

"Good."

I let my head fall back on the headrest, unable to hold it up any longer. Adrenaline had gotten me this far, but I needed blood. Stat. And not from Rick, who looked like a mosquito bite would push him over the edge.

"Rick, we've got a stop to make before you take me back."

"No way. Someone's going to notice you missing any time now."

"I doubt it," I muttered. "Either we stop for a drink or you're it," I said more loudly, reaching a hand over to squeeze his leg . . . hard. "Got it?"

He swallowed and turned, if possible, even paler, almost like a year-old vamp, all faded without the sun. "Where?" he asked.

"The mall. Where else?"

Back to my element. The mall was safe and sane, with all kinds of bright lights and sparklies and retail therapy. Lucky me, it would be on summer hours, open late, since we were past Memorial Day. It could even be that Marcy was headed there. It was instinctive, like salmon swimming upstream or knowing what skirt to pair with what blouse.

I watched out the window as Rick drove, thinking again about my old life. Would it really be so hard to return to it? Pull a big-screen entrance back at school in bitchin' heels and a skirt slit so high no one would be able to talk about anything else, including the fact that I was supposed to be dead? Why on earth should I go back to the compound?

Marcy was gone, and she wouldn't dare return to Melli's. No one else there would even speak to me. Well, okay, I'd felt the first chink in everyone's good-little-soldier armor tonight when they helped me escape to save Marcy. Chaz had even tossed me my boots. And then, of course, there was Bobby. I flashed on those baby blues of his, which could focus on me with that ego-boosting total attention, like I was the only thing in the world. Plus, the boy could kiss. I didn't even want to think about what kind of practice he'd had before me or the fact that Melli-noma was part of that.

On this side, there were mochachinos and malt balls— not that I could eat them anymore—Becca, Mom, and Dad …

"Turn here," I instructed.

"But this isn't the way to the mall. You said one stop," he protested.

"This isn't a stop. It's a drive-by." I didn't expect Mom and Dad to be home, and I wouldn't know what to say to them if they were, but I couldn't be this close and not check. Besides, Marcy's house was right down the road, on the corner of Jacoby and Pine, so I had a perfectly good excuse for passing by. She might have come this way, following the same homing instinct I hadn't known I had.

We never got as far as Pine. The lights at my house were blazing. My heart sank at the thought that it had only taken my folks a few days to forget about me and take back their lives. But then I noticed a police car parked half a block down the street, right in front of Bobby's abandoned POS that I'd forgotten all about.

I jumped at the idea that something else had called my parents back—like maybe the cops. Had Bobby and I left the side door open when we were ambushed? Had the place been robbed? Had someone been hurt?

I had the car door open and one foot out before Rick launched himself over me to grab the door handle and keep me from bolting. The car sped up and swerved wildly, and I had a flashback to the night of my death. Terrified, I jerked myself back and Rick slammed the door after me, regaining control.

"What was *that* all about?" he asked, still speeding so I wouldn't be tempted to throw myself out.

"That was my place."

"So?"

"There were police inside. I'm sure of it."

"And you were going to ... what? Let everyone see you? You don't think your parents would freak?"

I thought of Mom, who practically barricaded herself in the house when Mercury was in retrograde. She'd probably wig out at the sight of me. The thought hurt. Sure, I hadn't paid that much attention when I'd had them, when it wasn't like they were going anywhere, but now ... I thumped myself back in the seat, arms crossed. "Fine, the mall then. They have that stupid little sports café tucked back in a corner. Maybe I can preempt one of the TVs and tune it to local news."

"Are you kidding? The game'll be on. You'll start a riot." I growled.

"Department store electronics department. That's my final offer," he said.

I shrugged. "Whatever, but make it upscale. I need some new duds. This shirt reeks of blood." His, actually.

Rick gave me a look, which after the boogeyman just seemed laughable. "Your wish is my command, *princess*."

"So glad you've finally figured that out," I answered.

Rick found a shadowed section of underground parking garage and, with a little sprint, I caught a girl just getting into her Jetta. Rick watched the whole scene a bit too avidly, like he expected to see some girl-on-girl action, but all he witnessed was my donor turning to putty in my hands and sinking down into the driver's seat. Hot blood rushed into my mouth as I bit into her neck. I barely tasted it. I was all about the tingle, the fire rushing through my limbs, the heady strength and vitality flooding through me. My knees went weak with relief.

I let go when her head lolled to the side, suddenly afraid I'd taken too much. Fear goosed my heart. I reached down to feel her pulse, and she moaned, nearly scaring the bejeebers out of me. As gently as I could, I tucked her the rest of the way into the car and set her locks so no one could disturb her while she was out.

I waved Rick to me, like a valet who would carry the many bags I'd soon have. Even worried about my parents, the fresh blood and the sight of the mall put a little swing into my step.

"You can't just go in looking like yourself," Rick protested.

I looked down at myself... at the dusty, wrinkled clothes I'd been wearing for days, the stiff spot where Rick's lifeblood had gushed at me, my boots scuffed by running for my life. "Excuse me? I look like the fashionista of the damned. No one's going to recognize me. And if they do, just tell them I'm really my evil twin."

"Well, given this new look, I'm also worried about mall security."

"You can play lookout if you're so concerned. You see anyone, you cover me."

"How?"

"Strike up a conversation, head them off, something. Jeez, how did you ever get through junior high?"

Rick looked as if he'd like to throttle me, but I scooted inside where there were too many witnesses and led my way toward one of the superstores for both news and couture. I meant to hit the TVs first, I swear I did, but savvy store designers brought us in near the clothes and oooh... shiny. Satin called to me. And silk. And a teeny, tiny little kilt complete with buckles and matching knee socks that might just leave Bobby speechless.

Rick's comment about mall security had gotten to me, and I snuck into a dressing room as soon as I could with an armful of clothes, ordering Rick off to get me some shoes. "Size seven. No pastels."

He growled but he obeyed, rightly figuring, I guess, that it was the fastest way to get me out of the place.

Then he was gone, and I was surrounded by mirrors with no reflection to show for it. How was I ever going to know what looked good?

"Did you hear that?" asked a voice in the stall right next to me, and I froze halfway out of my bloody shirt.

"What?" A girl responded, a few dressing rooms down.

"That totally sounded like Gina!"

Becca . . . the ache that had started in my chest with the lights at my parents' place went critical.

"But she's *dead*."

"I know that, dork." Was the other voice Cindy McCallan? "But if she was going to, like, haunt someplace, don't you think it would be the mall?"

Cindy, if that's who it was, snorted. I'd always hated that about her. "You totally need to get over that already. She's gone, okay? You don't have to follow her lead anymore."

"I *am* over it," Becca said peevishly. "And she was always following *my* lead anyway."

I couldn't have breathed right then if I'd needed to. Mom and Dad back in less than a week . . . even maybe with good reason . . . Becca hanging with silly Cindy, famous for wearing Crocs with socks. Becca totally revising our entire history, *already over my death*. Was I that forgettable?

It cost me a huge effort to finish changing, but I was

hell-bent on escaping that changing room before the others. I didn't want to come face-to-face with my old life after all, if all I had left to love me was a Creamsicle-colored stuffed cat.

I didn't even pay much attention to what I put on—a glittery tank, some straight-legged jeans. I grabbed up everything else and bolted ... straight into Rick and his shoe boxes.

"There's something you need to see," he said ominously.

I bit my lip. Mom ... Dad ...

He pulled me and I jogged over to the electronics section. We both stopped dead in front of a large screen TV that sported Bobby's photo in the upper right hand corner.

"Turn up the sound!" I ordered Rick, and he did it without even an argument.

"—wanted for questioning in the disappearance of several bodies from local cemeteries. More bizarre, the suspect himself seems to have gone missing. Earlier this evening his car was discovered abandoned outside the home of the latest ... Brad, can she be called a victim if she's already dead?" the female anchor asked her co-host.

All the blood I'd just taken in drained to my stomach, forming a cold, hard lump. They couldn't really think Bobby was involved in the disappearances!

"I'm not sure what to call her, Helen. Apparently, the night watchman at Shady Pines Cemetery swears to seeing the girl walk out under her own steam. She was identified from this photograph." A photo of me replaced Bobby's in the upper right corner. My school picture from junior year. The year of the zit from hell and the one time my parents had forgotten to check the airbrushing option. My life was well and truly over.

"Speaking of steam, I hear this week's going to be a scorcher. Let's go to ..."

I tuned them out. "We've got to get back," I told Rick.

"Well, duh."

I led the way, going as fast as my boots would carry me. Alarms jangled as I left with my armful of clothes, security tags still attached, but I kept right on going. Those things went off so often by mistake that hardly anyone paid attention anymore, and I was too upset to care. Bobby had to know he was wanted for questioning so that he could clear his name ... or at least stay hidden away. I just hoped that if my parents had heard about the whole night-watchman thing they weren't freaking out. But if the polyester patrolman described what I'd been wearing ... well, they'd recognize it, right? There couldn't be two dresses that ugly in the world. And if the news of my bizarre reanimation was what had brought them back, not a robbery ... then maybe Fluffy wasn't the only one to care after all.

Rick got to the car first, being without spiked heels, and drove around to collect me before peeling out of the parking lot like a bat outta hell. He nearly ran down a pair of gangsta wannabees whose pants were in danger of sliding off their butts, revealing oh-so-sexy striped boxers.

· · ·

Rick let me off in the high school parking lot where he'd first picked me up.

"Sure you don't want to bite me and blow this Popsicle stand?" he asked before I'd escaped entirely.

I rolled my eyes. "I've always liked Popsicles. Besides, I have unfinished business." And besides again, while biting him didn't sound so bad, the idea of opening my vein in return was just gross, like week-old sweat socks.

"Well, I'll be here whenever Connor doesn't need me elsewhere or security doesn't chase me off. You know, just in case."

I looked at Rick—really looked at him. Gaunt, haggard, the skin sunken around his eyes. My defenses were so battered with all of the blows I'd taken tonight that I actually allowed myself to care.

"You all right?" I asked.

He shrugged and looked away, but I was glad for a chance to focus on someone else's issues.

"Rick?"

"Sure," he answered, voice brittle and bitter, "nothing a new kidney wouldn't fix. That's how she gets us, you know, the ones who can't afford to buck her and go running their mouths off. We have to take the crap she dishes out, hoping and praying to get vamped. Cured." Cured like the blond book-girl had been? If Rick knew about that—if he'd in fact instigated it, as I suspected—his position had to be totally unbearable. How desperate was his need for a kidney? I could almost understand him coming on so strong back at Melli's house of horrors. If his time was running out, subtlety might be a luxury he couldn't afford.

"You know, if you'd just told me all this right at the beginning instead of coming on all smarmy, I would have helped you out."

"How about now?"

Part of me really wanted to, but I didn't trust it. Maybe after this spark of … emotion … died down I'd be able to think clearly. "Can't right now. Until I know just what's what, and who to trust, I'm not creating some rogue vamp. But I'll tell you what. When this is all over and I get all our friends freed … and if you help with that …" I left the rest unspoken. It was the best I could do.

Hope sparked in his eyes but his lips twisted, like he'd bitten into a rotten apple. "How do I know *you're* not just stringing me along?"

I looked him dead in the eyes. "Ricardo Lopez, have you ever known me not to say exactly what was on my mind?"

He thought about that for a second. "No."

"Why would I start now?"

"Convenience," he answered, but not like he believed it. "Anyway, what have I got to lose? Like I said, I'll be here when I can in case you need me. Tell Connor about the watchdogs. I don't think they know about the trap door exit, but they've got eyes on all the others."

I nodded and shut my door. I didn't know what use I could make of Rick … yet. Part of me really wanted to call him back, to do the blood exchange thing just in case the damage Melli and her crew had done killed him before I could save him. But for all I knew he was putting me on. My moment of weakness had passed; he was going to have to prove himself before I gave him so much as a paper cut.

15

I got back in the same way I'd gotten out, though I had a heck of a time finding the secret passage from the outside end. I ended up rapping on the ground of, like, a square mile of woods before I finally got the passage to open. By the time I did, my spankin' new threads were nearly as filthy as my old. I wanted a long, hot shower to wash away the dirt and memories.

All of Team Alpha, which wasn't out on maneuvers, crowded around me as the trap door slid back. It was like a balm to my soul.

"Where's Marcy?" Pam and Vanessa asked in unison.

"Safe," I answered, struggling to keep my bag of new duds clean in one hand, while pulling myself up the ladder with the other.

"Safe where—at the mall?" some boy asked, looking at my haul. I didn't recognize him from school, so I was thinking junior or sophomore. His dark hair was buzzed perilously close to his skull.

"Yeah," I said wryly. "She's playing mannequin. Hiding in plain sight."

I despaired of him completely when he accepted that for an answer. As the trap door shut behind me, Cassandra leaned in.

"Where, really?" she asked quietly.

I was spared having to answer when the double doors burst open and Thing One and Thing Two, also known as the beefcakes, stood in the entrance.

"Gina," Thing One called. Just one name, like "Pink" or "Madonna."

The folks gathered around me stayed put, not fading back out of the way as they had before. They might even have tightened formation.

"What do you want with her?" Cassandra challenged.

Things One and Two exchanged a look, at which the latter huffed and said, "Relax, she'll be back."

And I would, too. I'd beaten death and a hell of a scary psychic already. Everything else was cake.

"Thanks," I told Cassandra quietly. "I've got this. Watch these for me?"

She turned, looking completely unsure, but took the clothes I handed her.

I stepped gently past my protectors, touched that they'd stood between me and Melli's goons even for a second. I felt like the Grinch—not in the Seussical green and wrinkly way with bad teeth and no pants, but in the sense that it felt like my heart grew three sizes. I had real friends, people willing to shield me from the big bad. Maybe this new life didn't entirely suck rocks, despite Melli-noma and her merry band of misfits...

Who all seemed to be waiting for me in what must have been a combat training room, all padded walls pocked with cuts and bruises. Bobby was standing wild-eyed in the middle. There was a chair there too, a single, gunmetal gray folding chair, into which Thing One pushed me.

"Don't move," he ordered.

I glanced at the guys looming behind Bobby: Hawkman, who was looking completely psychotic and intensely focused, testing the blades of the knives strapped across his chest like Rambo's answer to the pageant sash; and Larry, who was holding a sword and looking weirdly comfortable with it, like maybe he conducted mock D&D battles on the weekends. I felt like a nine-year-old called on to play the target in a stage show where the guy with the blades had the shakes. Then there was the dragon lady in the even deeper background, way back in a corner, where she could watch with minimal chance of collateral damage. Tonight she had on totally kick-ass leather pants that fit her like a second skin, and a scarlet top that came to a V so deep there had to be serious fashion tape keeping her puppies in place.

"*Now* there will be no holding out on me," Mellisande said, venom practically dripping from her lips.

"But I'm not telekinetic!" Bobby protested, turning to her in horror. "Not so you'd notice, anyway. I can't move anything heavier than a pencil!"

I wasn't sure that was entirely true, not based on his excitement when he'd told me about his power. I couldn't fault him for holding out on her, but from the tension in the room, I was kind of afraid to ask what had happened to the last target. I couldn't imagine Bobby letting someone get killed, but deflecting the goon's blades enough to save me without alerting Melli still meant pain and blood I could only recently afford to lose. No way did I want my person pierced.

"Well, then, you'd better learn, and damned fast. If you fail to stop the metal blades, I'll be forced to resort to the fire-hardened wood. She won't come back quite as easily from that … if at all. Or I can simply have Larry swing for the throat. It's been years since I've attended a good beheading."

Melli was going *down*. Meanwhile, I made a mental note of these sure-fire methods of vamp vanquishing, for when the time came.

"If you can't control the weapons, control the minds," she offered as a tip.

The beefcakes took up their positions as well. The model pulled a flip blade from his back pocket, and the professor faded back beside Melli, the better to analyze the action, maybe. So, counting the goons, it was three against one, with the possibility of two more joining in.

Bobby's eyes met mine, and I could see him trying to find a way out for me. It had to be hard enough controlling three people without trying to be subtle on top of it ... and the dragon lady had just taken that option away.

She didn't give him any time to think of another. "Go!" she ordered.

As one, Hawkman, Larry, and Thing One all flew into action. Hawkman launched one of his throwing knives a half-second before Larry and the Thing lunged at me, bloodlust in their eyes. Larry gave an inarticulate battle cry, less Conan the Barbarian than Warrior Princess. My eyes squeezed shut instinctively, and I braced for impact ... and braced ...

The lack of pain seemed almost anticlimactic. I opened one eye, then the other. Before me, frozen in mid-air, were the weapons. The throwing knife hovered for an instant before dropping to the floor. The flip knife and sword did the same, their wielders struggling to lift them as if they now weighed a ton.

Mellisande laughed. It was nasty, but not the skittering chill of her psychic's amusement. "Good boy," she said. "You just needed the proper motivation."

"Screw you," Bobby spat.

"Perhaps another time," she agreed.

"Bitch," I snarled.

"The kind that will rip your throat out soon as look at you," she answered. "And don't you forget it."

She twitched a hand and without warning, Thing Two, the professor, pulled some things out of his jacket. It was so fast that I couldn't even see what they were before they were flying at me. Bobby, distracted, released the other weapons to stop the new threat, and the room erupted again. Only Larry, screaming bloody murder, was swinging for Bobby. I was paralyzed by indecision. Should I cry out a warning and risk distracting Bobby, fly into action myself and risk the same (since he could only focus on where he expected me to be), or freeze? But there wasn't even enough time to think it out. One of the professor's throwing stars caught me in the shoulder and I flinched, narrowly avoiding the other one.

Bobby ducked the sword and whirled, one arm flung out to knock the throwing knife coming at me out of the air with a burst of power that also shattered Thing One's flip knife. Larry recovered from his missed swing and launched himself again at Bobby, at the same time Thing One switched targets, ready to throttle Bobby with his bare hands, one bleeding from the explosion of his blade.

Bobby let out a sound like a cornered grizzly bear and shot such a blast of power through the room that my hair stood on end. My skin tingled and pricked, like from a really invigorating body wrap, and everything in the room *froze*. Nothing was stirring, not even a mouse. I tested my limbs, but could only blink.

Mellisande's glee, frozen on her face, slowly melted off, and I realized she was fighting the power. Her lips, when she spoke, were tight, as if she were in a mud mask that had dried solid and her face might crack if she moved. "I *own* you," she said out loud.

But then Bobby flinched, his face twisting like he'd suddenly been struck with brain freeze. His mouth came open as if to gasp, but his lungs weren't holding any air. Sweat, red as blood, glistened at his hairline.

Slowly, so slowly, the rest of the room started to move as Bobby lost focus, tied up in some kind of mental struggle for control with his dam.

Hawkman had another knife ready to throw and Thing Two another star when Bobby fell to one knee, clutching his head. Time sped up again.

"Enough," Melli said, triumphant. This time everyone paused on her say-so. "Take the girl back. The boy and I have much to discuss."

I reached up to pull the throwing star out of my shoulder, letting the spurt of blood from it clean the wound. I wanted to hurl the star at the dragon lady so badly I could taste it, but with my luck she'd just mind-control one of her minions to take the bullet or whatever. Not that I had any warm and fuzzy feelings toward most of them, but what if she picked Bobby? Plus, I had the feeling I'd only piss her off. She might even try to control me, and my one and only edge—my resistance to her mesmerism—might be discovered before it could do me any good. I let the star fall to the ground and met Bobby's pain-filled eyes as Things One and Two once again pulled me from the room. I could tell from the look on Bobby's face that he felt he'd failed. I mouthed that it was okay, but he closed his eyes and shook his head in denial of my message.

16

The next night, the house was in an uproar. None of us belowstairs knew what was happening, not at first, but shortly after sunset the doorbell rang, and a few minutes later came the cry of a scorned woman. Then there was a lot of running to and fro, and some slamming of doors. Neither Alpha nor Beta teams were called out.

After the events of the past few nights, the mood in the dorm was tense. Some kids played cards, others talked or tried to read the spotty magazines, but deep down everyone listened.

A couple of underclass girls approached me, kind of shyly, as if they might scatter if I said "boo." The shorter of the two spoke when I looked up, after taking in a gasp of air. "Uh, hey. Um, Marcy had said she'd braid our hair tonight and her being, um, away, we were wondering if maybe you—"

I grabbed onto her like a lifeline and she nearly jumped out of her skin. "Well, thank God. I'm going so nuts wondering what's going on up there that I was about to do something *crazy*. Sit."

I pulled the thin foam pillow off my bed and threw it to the floor so she could sit in comfort. A tremulous smile formed on her face. "I'm Katie, and this is Di."

"Hi. Gina, but I guess you've heard."

"Yeah, kinda," she admitted. "Did you really sleep with the entire football team?"

I was going to *kill* Tina Carstairs … with metal, so she'd heal and I could kill her again. "You've got me confused with someone else," I said sweetly.

"Oh." She blushed. "Sorry."

"Sit," I ordered.

Her friend Di produced a brush, and I might have been a little—vigorous—at first with the strokes, but after a while it was kind of soothing to work on her hair. It was thick and a really pretty shade of chestnut that went with her brown eyes. The freckles … well, concealer could take care of those, maybe take her from cute to junior-league hottie, especially with some sun-kissed copper on her lips and cheeks, maybe some highlights. On the other hand, the freckles kind of worked for her. "What do you want?" I asked. "French braid? Inverted braid? Weave?"

"Um, whatever?"

And she'd *definitely* have to lose the "um."

I gave her a double braid into a classic bun. Made Katie look like a prima ballerina. It wouldn't have been my thing, but it made her look dainty and polished rather than just cute, which everyone knew was a four-letter word meaning "let's be friends."

Di was next, but she had kind of sharp features and a braid would totally be too severe. She'd look like the kind of librarian you just didn't cross.

"What about a cut?" I asked.

Di shifted from foot to foot. "Like what?"

"I'm thinking bangs. You've got such a high forehead, some bangs would totally soften you up."

"Um…"

I looked her in the eyes. "You going to wear the same hair for all eternity?"

She scrunched her face at me, but plopped down on the pillow her friend had vacated.

"Anyone got scissors?" I yelled out.

I looked up and found we'd gathered a mini-audience of girls forming a rough line-up where Di had been standing.

"Cuticle," offered one of the girls.

"Anything else?" I asked hopefully.

Everyone looked to everyone else, but there wasn't a set of shears to be found.

"Cuticle it is then," I said, thanking the girl who offered them.

It wasn't easy, and I practically had to go strand by strand, but eventually, Di had fairly credible-looking bangs. I fluffed them a little around her face, pushing the bulk of them off to the right in a flirty asymmetrical look, and changed the center part of her hair to do the same. She looked like a whole 'nother person.

"Tomorrow, makeup," I said, brooking no argument.

She nodded and practically bounced off to get second and third opinions, since mirrors were totally useless.

"Me next?" asked a girl with a really heinous page boy cut. Even Catherine Zeta Jones had a tough time pulling that one off in *Chicago*. Page boys should have been outlawed ages ago, along with beehives, mullets, and faux-hawks—that cut for guys who weren't edgy enough to commit to the full mohawk, which unless you were punk was another iffy look in my book.

"You trust me?" I asked.

She turned on the pillow to study me. "Maybe?"

"Close enough," I said. "Turn."

And before she could think twice, I started clipping. "Flinch and I'm likely to nick an ear," I told her. Not that it was the kind of threat it could have been, if she'd still been human with only natural healing abilities.

I gave her a really modern, spiky pixie cut. She looked

totally mod now, like she could go out and start her own band.

I smiled, almost able to forget where I was and why. Gina Covello, beautifying the world one girl at a time.

Then those double doors opened again—trouble every time. This time Bobby stood there, flanked by nearly Mellisande's entire entourage.

"You've got two minutes," she told him.

I rose and stepped over the girl who'd dropped to take the pixie's place.

"Gina," he breathed, meeting me halfway but holding me only by my hands so that he could see my face, like he was trying to memorize it. "I have to go. They're sending me"—he looked back over his shoulder toward the dragon lady, and not with longing—"somewhere, for a while. I wouldn't leave without saying good-bye."

The council. I was sure of it. Melli-noma was handing him over. But why? If she was plotting something, as everything here seemed to indicate, wouldn't she want him with her rather than against her?

"When will you be back?" I asked.

He pulled me to him then and held me. I breathed in that musky scent that was him and gripped him tightly. "I don't know." *But I'll try to get you word,* he said in my head. *I'm not sure how far my power will extend.*

I tried not to react, but it stunned me senseless. I wondered how long *that* power had been developing. With Connor thinking hot toddies at me and the freakshow psychic crawling like critters through my mind, I might as well hang out a "For Rent" sign and get something out of the whole deal.

Knock first next time, I thought back at him, not certain I wanted him to hear. The one-way ticket was one thing, but I wasn't actually sure how I felt about a boyfriend who could read my mind. My mouth alone got me into enough trouble.

He kissed me then and it was practically one of the great screen kisses of all time … like MJ and Spiderman, only right side up. Bobby would love that thought, and I kinda had to wonder if it was for certain my own because I wasn't usually big with the superhero references. Though, in my defense, Tobey Maguire did have totally hot blue eyes. But I wasn't really thinking of Tobey Maguire then … or, not much anyway. Bobby was nipping at my lower lip, nuzzling my nose with his, his hands practically like claws down my back. I could totally remember exactly how I'd gotten into trouble with him at the after-prom party. The boy was hot!

"That's enough," the dragon lady cut in, sounding really peeved. "You've said your good-bye."

Only Bobby didn't pay her any attention. She snapped, and I felt him stiffen all over. Slowly, unwillingly, he left me to go to her.

Larry and Hawkman each took an arm before Bobby could buck her control.

Having been shanghaied the second I got back from

rescuing Marcy to play the target in Melli-noma's sadistic games, I hadn't had the chance to report anything at all to Connor. I could only hope he sought me out tonight, because I wanted some answers myself. This had all gone too far. Kids dying to become Melli's Merry Minions was bad enough. Kids like Marcy permanently disappearing— in theory if not in actuality—was another thing altogether. The dragon lady had given me way too many reasons not to trust her. She was playing a dangerous game with this mysterious council—keeping secrets, building an army, stockpiling weapons. I didn't want my friends to be cannon fodder in whatever war was brewing, and I was not excited about my boyfriend being on the front lines.

The line-up for my amateur beautician services still hung uncertainly around my cot, but I'd lost focus. When Connor called me out, like, an *hour* later, my nerves were totally shot. I was starting to seriously consider nailbiting as a hobby.

"What did you learn?" he asked right away, as soon as he had me in the dungeon area where Bobby and I had necked just a few nights before.

I hit him. I don't know who was more surprised, him or me. It was only a blow to the arm, but still . . .

"How could you let her send Bobby away?" I asked, not at all liking the needy quality of my voice.

He narrowed his eyes at me. "It's all part of the plan. Don't worry, he won't be there long."

"What does that mean?" I asked, liking the belligerent note a lot better.

"It means that Bobby's presence with the council will open doors." *Just like in the prophecy*, I thought. "That's all I will say on the matter. Now—"

"And all that running around we heard earlier tonight—what was that about?"

He snarled. "Tell me—" I could feel him try to compel me, but it was like a gentle wave compared to Bobby's tsunami of power.

I waited for him to remember. "No," I said.

"Fine," he spat. "We received a *gift* from the council that convinced us to move up our timetable."

"What?" I asked, not at all liking the freaky emphasis on *gift*.

His eyes gleamed with sadistic glee. "Someone I think you might know—part of her, anyway. She'd been scalped."

"Marcy?" I asked in horror.

Rick had said the council was watching. They must have seen Melli's goons take Marcy and been waiting with open arms when she escaped the psycho-psychic. I'd only managed to send her from the frying pan into the fire. My knees nearly buckled, but then I realized ... as a vampire, she could probably totally heal from a scalping, although it was, like, a fate worse than death; Marcy would be devastated. She also, either from torture or compulsion, would have told them everything they wanted to know about smelly Melli's setup, which had to be the message the council was sending with her scalp.

"It was a summons. Mellisande *will* appear to swear fealty to the council and bind her and hers to the council or she will be crushed."

"But just swearing—"

"It is not so simple as that. The ritual is binding. Now—" Like a bird of prey, he swooped in to grab my arms, hard enough to bruise. *"Tell. Me."* There was no power behind it this time, just a clear physical threat. I wasn't afraid, but I *was* finished with him.

"Bobby is what matters, okay? He's, like, some kind of key." *And I'm chaos*, I thought, *hear me roar.* "You said he'd open doors. Well, the psychic said the same."

"So, Mellisande will prevail?" he asked.

I shrugged. "He didn't say so specifically. Just something about the boy who debates holding the universe in his hands, unlocking doors and causing change."

"That's it? Nothing else?" His grip on me was tightening.

I huffed. "Have you ever tried talking to this guy? He's like Ted Bundy, Hannibal Lecter, and the BTK Killer all wrapped into one, only without the charm. And his breath—I mean, would it kill him to gargle?"

Connor looked like he'd totally gotten the short end of the information stick.

"You're sure?" he asked.

"He also did a lot of calling me *morsel* and *pretty pretty pretty* and trying to eat me."

Weirdly, Connor looked a lot more comfortable at that, like he was at last sure we were talking about the *same* psychopath. "Fine, the *key*," he said, staring into space. "Agent of change." He wasn't talking to me anymore. Not really. I had ceased to exist.

"Can I go?" I asked.

He waved me away like a gnat, and I rubbed my nose with the certain finger teachers and parents take offense to. He never noticed.

Back in the dorm, I paused before letting the doors close behind me. They opened just fine from the hallway side, but not so much from the inside. I could march everyone out right flippin' now if only I had a place for them to hole up come dawn. Or I could lead them on a march against the council ... if only I knew how to find it. Maybe Rick—? But his car wouldn't hold everybody, not all at once, and I couldn't be sure he'd be there when I needed him, or that he wouldn't tattle.

Wistfully, I let the door close. We could always escape through the hatch if need be. But a plan would be nice.

I was almost instantly mobbed upon entrance.

"What's going on?" demanded Trevor, the ROTC guy who'd helped me with the hatch catch.

I looked up at him and don't know what my face showed, but he took a half step back. "That bad?"

"The council has Marcy ... and Bobby."

Silence.

"The council?" Di asked tentatively. She really did look way better with the bangs.

Oh right, the council; the kids totally weren't in the know on all that. I made a quick decision.

"Okay, everybody, sit," I ordered, moving away from the door so they'd do the same. The way sound bounced around in here, I hoped no one would be able to make out actual words even if they did listen in, but I wasn't taking any chances.

"Ooh, story time," Tina sing-songed.

"Bite me entirely," I shot back.

"In your dreams," she sneered.

"No, in yours."

Her mouth opened and shut like a carp but no comeback emerged. I air-scored myself a point and sat down on one of the cots. People settled around me. I looked from one face to another, trying to read them to see if anybody looked like a snitch or teacher's pet... besides Tina. I wouldn't put anything past her, but if I could make her *see*... if I could make them all see...

"Listen. Mellisande, much as she may play it, is not the be-all and end-all of vamps. There's a council, and Mellisande is on their hit list. They want to crush her; she wants to take them over. We're going to get caught in the middle."

"Or maybe," Tina broke in, "we kick major ass, end up on the winning team, and live like queens."

I gave her a *look*. "Let's think. So far, have you been treated like (a) honored guests or (b) inmates? I mean, sure there's no homework and you get room and board, but what's with all this Alpha and Beta nonsense?"

"Exercise," she answered. "You might want to try it sometime."

"Some of us are blessed with a naturally high metabolism," I told her sweetly. Actually, I hadn't been able to so much as look at chocolate since puberty without paying for it at the gym, but she didn't have to know that.

The double doors opened again and everyone glanced guiltily at them, like we were doing something wrong just talking, something that might lead to punishment. I think that did more than anything to shoot down Tina's happily-ever-after fantasy.

"Team Alpha, you're up," Larry said, striding into the room with Chickzilla. "Gina, today you're joining up."

"But I don't—"

"Have anything better to do," the Chick finished for me. If I didn't know any better, I'd think she was trying to save me from myself.

I rolled my eyes at her but took the cue. I figured, worst-case scenario, I'd shoot an eye out in a paintball tussle. It would grow back. Best case, maybe I'd get some kind of clue about what-all was going on. At least I wouldn't be brooding myself into a wrinkly mess.

The Chick and Larry did their "complicated" little rhythm on the door and we marched off into the tunnel like the seventeen little dwarves. Once in, the Chick unlocked a cabinet I hadn't noticed in my previous rush to get through to Marcy and brought out weapons, a whole mess of them. She and Larry handed out bows as we filed past, but kept the arrows for themselves in slings across their backs. They then pulled on knapsacks bulging with something else entirely, though I had no idea what, and wrestled out two targets shaped like upper torsos with heads instead of the standard archery rounds. I looked around at the others, but no one else reacted to the targets, which had to mean they'd seen them before. They totally gave me the creeps.

The tunnel spat us out, as expected, at the Mozulla High School athletic fields. It was a good thing the school's budget didn't allow for nighttime security and it was way too late for any actual teams to be using the area, which was sheltered from any drive-by traffic by the other buildings and the treeline.

To start, Chickzilla pulled me aside—way, way downfield, apparently not trusting my aim. I looked back at the others, and Larry was dividing them into three groups and handing out ... guns? ... to one set. I thought about Marcy's paintball-splotched cami, but these looked more like water guns, which was totally surreal. Another group got pointy sticks and the third lined up before the other target.

"Earth to Gina," Chickzilla said, knocking on my head with her knuckles. "You need to focus."

I glared. "What I *need* is a mani-pedi and a lifetime

supply of moisturizer. This blood-only diet isn't exactly hydrating."

"Well, princess, I won't argue you there. But if you have any sense of self-preservation, you'll let me teach you how to shoot."

"Fine, whatever."

Before she handed me the bow, she demonstrated how to hold it in my left hand—firmly, but not so firmly there wasn't any give.

I gave it a try. Ooh, holding...difficult. Chickzilla's hand lashed out, almost vampire fast, and knocked the bow from my hand.

"Tighter than *that*," she told me.

I glared. "I wasn't ready."

"Then get ready. And *fast*."

"Why?"

But she only shook her head and retrieved my bow, handing it to me again. I held it tighter, until I thought I heard the wood start to groan and eased up.

"Now..." She showed me how to hold the string between my first and second fingers right at the first knuckle and how to aim. There was only one problem.

"Um, Chick?"

She gave me a really funny look, and I realized she probably had an actual *name*.

"Carrie," she corrected me.

"You're kidding?" I looked at her dead on, figuring

an evil minion should have a way tougher name, like... I don't know, Charlie or Max or *Chickzilla*.

She glared.

"Okay, okay. If it was good enough for Stephen King—"

"What?" she asked tightly.

"What-what?" I answered.

"You had a question?"

"Oh, right. Um, what do I do about the boobs?"

"What?" she asked again.

"You know—chest, bazooms, jugs, hooters." My eyes fell to her unitard, "Oh, uh, maybe you don't know."

She snarled and did a pretty decent job of it.

"If you're worried, you can bind them," she hissed.

I grimaced. "Never mind."

She shrugged, handed me an arrow, and made a production of getting far far out of the way, like behind me and way to the side.

"Now, nock the arrow, lay the front of the shaft along the sight line, pull back on the tail until it's level with the corner of your mouth, aim, and let fly."

I did and howled with pain, dropping everything to the ground. The arrow flew, but not far, considering it had left part of itself behind, embedded in *my finger*.

Brightly colored faux feather taunted me, sticking out of my finger like a gaudy splinter.

I expected the Chick's face to be smug, but instead it held a wince. "Been there, done that. You'll heal," she said, plucking the feather from me and ignoring my "Yipe!" of pain. "You need to release quickly and all at once. Don't be tentative."

I was *tentatively* considering mutiny, but since now was not the time or place, I did my best to learn the really ancient way of getting rid of an enemy. I was no fan of guns, but wooden bullets would have been a ton easier— though I guess ordering them would raise some eyebrows, and they probably aren't too aerodynamic.

I totally did a lot better with the water guns, having practiced with the hair spray against psycho-psychic. I was guessing that in the event of an actual emergency, they'd be filled with holy water or garlic water or something equally toxic. The hand-to-hand with the pointy sticks … well, the less said about that the better. They actually turned out to be, like, plastic tent stakes—I guess to avoid any of us dusting each other accidentally or on purpose. Tina, her natural viciousness coming out, was actually pretty decent, so it was a good thing she and I never got paired up.

It felt like the longest gym class ever. By the time Chick-zilla called a halt, I was starving again, practically ready to go for her throat, but I worried that attacking Melli's minion might just get me dusted—and then who would save everyone from fashion and other disasters? The Chick hung back and let Larry pass around little plastic water bottles he took from one of the knapsacks, filled with something so dark the lights around the athletic fields didn't penetrate it. Blood, I was guessing, and shuddered at the thought of drinking it at room temperature like a Yoohoo or something. It was totally barbaric. Still, my eyeteeth grew. It would barely be enough to take the edge off the hunger. Was this all everybody was getting? Was smelly Melli keeping them, like, on the edge of starvation? But no one seemed to mind—exhilarated from the workout, they probably just chalked up the tired to honest labor. I'd drunk my fill, though, from actual veins. I knew the difference.

Cringing, I sucked down my bottle in no time flat. Two, maybe three gulps, not thinking about the temperature or texture, which was so much ... thicker ... bottled. My eyeteeth just barely receded, and I started eying the Chick again—I just couldn't think of her as Carrie—for dessert. I wondered what her damage was that she, like Rick, would let herself get used. She looked healthy enough, aside from her fashion sense. Maybe Melli paid well.

She seemed to sense my stare and turned from watching the group to watching me. "Don't even think about it. Once Melli's plan comes through, you can drink your fill." She raised her voice a bit. "Then you can *all* drink your fill."

It was a powerful enticement, for me at least, and I noted she was careful not to say anything about the actual plan, assuming she even knew. I mean, if Mellisande kept Connor in the dark ...

We weren't even halfway back through the tunnel when the anvil fell on my head. Or, not an anvil—more like a baseball bat that suddenly struck a shattering blow and stirred up a swarm of killer bees that nested just inside my crushed skull. Then they *freaked*, stinging every twist and turn of my brain until it felt near to exploding. I fell into the body in front of me—male, female, I didn't know. It was there and then gone, not about to take the fall with me. There were screams, but they could have been mine.

The pain splintered my sanity, even my balance. I smacked the ground so hard I bounced, rocks and sticks cutting into me and my brain. The pressure was so intense I actually hoped to die. Prayed for it. There was so much pain, it couldn't all be mine.

And it wasn't. I knew it in that instant, but the truth came to me in a blinding flash. The world winked out and I was left with one truth—the insect invasion, the prying open of my skull—I'd felt those before.

Morsel? that Tiny Tim voice asked in my head. He sounded almost lost, as if he'd lashed out all unknowing and found me. I didn't answer, couldn't, and he roared *You! You led them to me!*

But I couldn't make any sense of it—not through the haze of pain. Unless…unless those watchers Rick had warned about had followed someone else, probably Marcy, straight to him. That would mean—*gah*, it was like thinking through razor blades—that *them* was the council, which meant—

His patience broke, and the bees seemed to swell. The stingers, the rage, ripped me apart. I dashed my head against the ground. If I had any thought at all it was to open my skull, let the pain out, but someone grabbed me. Or something. I couldn't see, couldn't *feel* except that my flesh was on fire. And on top of that my body was being held down, compressed, imprisoned, probably by someone trying to keep me from killing myself. I was sixteen million degrees and counting. The first case of spontaneous in-human combustion, ready to fry my good Samaritan along with me.

Gina! someone called. Or maybe not. Maybe it was all in my head. I couldn't hear over the buzzing in my brain.

Voices around me sounded like nothing but static.

Gina, what's happening? the someone said again. Bobby? In my head?

Morsel. Do you fear me now? the freakshow asked, drowning him out.

"No!" I cried out. Or didn't. My body was in flames, and I couldn't feel, couldn't think. "Wasn't. Me."

The bees suddenly hushed. *Then who?*

I couldn't rat Marcy out, not even to save myself. It wasn't really her fault.

"Get her inside!" someone ordered.

With a roar of frustration, rage, and bloodlust, the freakshow tore my brain in half looking for the answer I refused him.

17

I came to with my teeth buried in Chickzilla's arm and Melli's smelly minions—no, wait, smelly Melli's minions—staring down at me. I slowly withdrew my fangs, lifting a shaky hand to brush at the corners of my mouth.

The dragon lady pushed the others aside. "What happened?" she demanded unsympathetically.

The Chick's blood had just saved my unlife, brought me back from another, surer death ... I thought so, anyway ... and Melli wanted to subject me to interrogation? That was wrong on so many levels. There were things I had to hide; I knew that much. I just had to remember what they were. For one, I couldn't let on that I'd ever met tall, dark, and demented. But I also had to find a way to let her know the psycho-psychic wasn't her ace in the hole anymore. If she was counting on him for intel in her war games, she'd be sadly disappointed. Maybe even enough to call the games off, especially when she considered all the tales he might have to tell the council.

"Something hit me like ... like a tidal wave. Something powerful, lashing out. Looking for *you*," I improvised, only half lying through my teeth.

She stared at me, not buying it. "I didn't feel anything."

"Whatever it was seemed ... disoriented, I guess, like something had gone really wrong."

"This *thing*," she said skeptically, "what did it feel like?"

That one was easy. "Like an army of insects invading my brain."

That got her attention. So nice to know I wasn't the only one ever to get the royal treatment. She obviously recognized my description.

"What did he say?" she asked sharply, and several of her lieutenants, or whatever they were, shot her a look like they also noticed the sudden change in her tone.

"The council has him, and man is he *pissed*."

Her face froze. If she'd had any color beyond her war paint, it would have drained away.

"Mellisande, what is it?" Connor asked.

She turned to him, her eyes blank for a moment before

she shook off her reaction. "Nothing. Just this child trying to make herself important with her lies."

I gaped. "Don't listen to her. If they can get any sense out of him, they'll *know*!" I practically shouted.

Her gaze latched onto mine like she was a starving hawk and I was a three-legged mouse. No chance for escape. Crap, crap, crap. I'd given something away. She now knew *I knew* more than I was saying, but she couldn't call me on it after branding me a liar.

"Take her away." Man, I was getting tired of hearing that. *Not the dungeon, not the dungeon,* I chanted to myself.

"To the dungeon?" Chickzilla echoed.

"Fine. Anywhere, just get her out of my sight."

The Chick helped me to my feet. It was totally pitiful that only a single human was needed to escort me, but I was still all woozy and walking wounded, like the morning after one of Marcy's punch parties. All the vamps stayed behind ... to argue, it sounded like, because before the door even shut I heard someone ask, "What aren't you telling us?"

Gina? Someone said in my head, softly. I winced.

"You okay?" Chickzilla asked, her hand gripping my elbow, half support and half shackle.

I looked up at her—jeez, she was a giant.

"Yeah ... thanks. Thanks for, ah, saving me."

She shrugged.

Bobby? I asked the mental voice. Did it make you crazy if you talked back to the voices in your head?

Gina, he said again, with a tone of such relief that it warmed my heart. *It seemed like you were under attack earlier.*

I shuddered. *Melli's psychic. The council has him, and he thought I gave him up.*

He got to you from here? Bobby asked, already growing fainter, like someone had turned his volume way down.

You did, I said ... thought ... whatever.

No answer.

Bobby?

Nothing. Not a whisper, not a word. If I was the kind of girl given to panic attacks, I'd probably be imagining all kinds of things, like the council bursting in on him, ticked off to find him communicating with the outside world, or imprisonment, torture ... but I wasn't that kind of girl. It was probably just, uh, his power needing to be recharged. It was all new to him. Probably he just had to work it, like a muscle. Build up to the heavy lifting.

"Gina?" Chick said, like it wasn't the first time.

"What?" I focused on her, on where I was, not on the stuff going on in my head.

"We're here and you didn't fight me once. No smart-ass comments, even. You sure you're okay?"

She almost sounded concerned.

I gave her a wobbly smile. "You do know that unitards have kind of jumped the shark, right?"

She blinked. "Sorry I asked. *In*," she said, opening the cell.

If I'd had the strength God gave a flea I might have made a run for it, but as it was, I meekly settled onto the bunk.

"Don't let the bed bugs bite," she said, shutting the door.

In this place I wasn't entirely sure it was a joke.

Anyway, Mellisande got a crack at me before the bed bugs. She came alone, which I could understand, but she'd given me time to think, which I couldn't. I mean, I might not have Bobby's debate club training, but I'd had plenty of experience arguing my way from an F to a D, and my earlier fog had blown away.

"Now," Melli said, as if I was going to be intimidated by her, after *him*, "you're going to give me the full story. What did you mean by 'if they can get any sense out of him, *they'll know*?' *You* already seem to know a lot more than you should."

I prepared to give the performance of my life—eyes wide, face baffled. "About *what?*" I asked. "Some creepy… guy… plays with my head and suddenly *I'm* the bad guy… girl… whatever. I only said the 'sense' thing 'cause the guy was totally all, like, backward talking and everything, like the love child of Yoda and Hannibal Lecter, you know?"

I flitted my hands around vaguely for good measure. She already thought I was a total ditz; I could work with that. But now she was studying me really hard, and I felt a puff of power shoot over me like I was a windshield. It didn't have nearly the force of Bobby's, but I could tell it was supposed to do *something*. If only I knew what—make me tell the truth? Cluck like a chicken? What?

I decided on the first one and let my voice go all, like, deadly dull while I retold my story, every word the sick psychic had spoken. In excruciating detail. It didn't take long, and then there was silence while Melli-noma thought until I could practically hear the gears grinding.

"They're going to see us coming," she murmured to herself.

I pretended not to hear, but I'd had the same thought. If psycho-psychic talked, out of revenge or simple hunger, Mellisande would lose the element of surprise, assuming she'd ever had it. Unless she had the council out-thought or outmanned, which I doubted, it would be a slaughter.

"I need to think about this," she said, rising.

"What about me?" I asked, trying to sound like I was snapping out of her whammy.

She turned. "I can't have you blabbing about this, alarming everyone."

"I won't!" I promised.

"No, you won't." I felt another zing of her power, but it didn't do a thing for me.

Still, I snapped my mouth shut and didn't say another word as she turned and walked away.

Now that I was "silenced," I expected Chickzilla or one of the other guards to set me free, bring me back to the others, but it didn't happen.

Not even Connor came to pick my brain, probably

too caught up in the dragon lady's war council or whatever. I wished I had Bobby's powers so I could maybe tap into Melli's mind and find out what was going on there. She couldn't be thinking of going against the council *now*, could she? If I were her ... okay, I wouldn't admit defeat, but maybe I'd keep the future murky by not deciding on a plan until the last second, which would only work if the future wasn't set in stone. But if that were the case, how could anyone "see" it? My brain hurt just thinking about it, and I lay down to let the dawn sweep me away.

It was a shame I hadn't had any dreams since I'd vamped out. Dreams are supposed to be your mind's way of telling you stuff. Right then, I would have taken all the clues I could get.

18

It wasn't until the next night, hours after the sun had set and I was about to go barking mad with boredom, that Connor actually showed his face. I was so desperate for distraction I was actually glad to see him. At least he was in a button-up shirt and pressed pants. He didn't look like he was about to go all commando, so probably the raid or scuffle or whatever with the council wasn't planned for tonight.

"What really happened last night?" he asked, without preamble.

"Unh-uh. You first, or you won't tell me anything. What's going on?"

"That's what I'm trying to figure out. Last night you really rocked Mellisande. Today she thinks she's found the perfect distraction. What gives?"

He could have been speaking Swahili for all the sense it made to me. Distraction? Unless … unless she was thinking of having Bobby use his powers and free the freakshow to distract the council from whatever she had planned. It made horrible, perfect sense. That thing loose in the council quarters would be total chaos. But would he care about or even notice the difference between friend and foe when we came to call?

"But—" But what? What was I going to say? "Listen, the council's got Melli's freakshow psychic all locked up. I think they followed her goons when they brought Marcy as a sacrifice. I don't know how their watchdogs missed me, but I'm sure I softened the psycho up for them. The council's going to see you coming, whatever you've got planned."

Connor chewed on that, forgetting my presence in a way that was getting far too familiar. I'd been ignored more over the past week than in probably the whole rest of my life combined.

"Look, if you hate the lady so much, why don't *you* just sneak out to the council and make your own deal?" It was out of my mouth before I realized the stupidity of it. If anybody should be sneaking out to cut a deal … but not unless I knew we'd be better off than we were now, and not without the others. Somehow or other, it seemed the entire group of kids had gotten under my skin. I'd already lost one family—I wasn't about to lose another. And based on Marcy's scalping—

"Never mind, forget I said anything."

"I've thought about it, actually," he said, surprising me with actual conversation. "But if I tell them what Mellisande's got planned, they'll run her over, absorb everyone they don't kill, and I'll be no better off. Maybe they'll set me up in her place, maybe not. I don't trust them."

So he could either help Melli succeed and continue to be her right-hand man, or he could make sure she went down in such a way that he could pick up the reins. If he went to the council with something—a territory, like, and a following—he could bargain from a position of strength. But where did that leave Bobby and Marcy, who just *had* to still be alive, and all the rest of us?

"When is it?" I asked. "She's going up against them, right? All-out war."

He studied me, not sure how much to say, but it was way too late for discretion. "Tomorrow. It has to be. That's when she's set to swear fealty."

Great. No time, no plan, and no freedom. I was screwed.

"So, I'm just going to be left here to rot?" I asked.

"Someone will be along in a bit. You're training again with Team Alpha. Say nothing," he ordered, his eyes drilling into mine as if he'd impose it by sheer force of will, since the mesmerism thing didn't work out.

Don't ask, don't tell. Sheesh, if I'd wanted to join the military I'd ... well, it was too crazy even to contemplate. At least I was getting sprung.

It was Larry who came to get me, Larry who stayed in the dorm to flirt with the bookish blond girl while I trudged off down the tunnel with Team Alpha for fun and games.

I missed Bobby, and I was tired of having my life directed for me. I had one night to save the, er, day ... a plan would have been good. Instead, I'd be busy trying not to get stabbed, sprayed, or shot. I blamed my sucky hand-to-hand skills on my distraction. Yup, just a day in the life of a typical teen ... only instead of dodging gossip and pop quizzes, it was stakes and spritzing. Gossip, at least, had never frizzed my hair.

19

The sun set and I burst awake, flailing like I was falling and trying to catch myself. I didn't remember dreaming, but it certainly hadn't been the peaceful sleep of the dead. Maybe my brain was trying to tell me something, like that the bottom was about to drop out of my world.

I was craving a mochachino in the worst way ... or the blood of a caffeine addict, I wasn't picky. Just a little pick-me-up so I didn't feel as old as, like, the chick with the frozen face who did the fashion wrap-ups on *E!*

Chickzilla, Sparky, and Hawkman moved around calling

everyone to attention and handing out mini-bottles of blood. *Their own?* I wondered, totally creeped out by the idea. I don't know why it hadn't occurred to me to wonder that before. But on second thought, no way could they spare so much. Maybe one of them had a day job at the hospital or blood bank.

I got dressed like everyone else, though some had farther to go than others. It was a good thing I'd made that stop at the mall with Rick, because my spiky-heeled boots and short skirt just weren't Rambo material. Closest thing I had were my new purple cross-trainers (which, of course, had no heels to speak of, and made me feel ridiculously short), and black, skin-tight jeans. It had killed me to forego color while shopping, but I'd grabbed a scoop-neck T-shirt in basic black in case I needed to sneak out again. Not that the cat-burglar look would do me much good against vampire senses. It was more of a state of mind, a dress-for-success mentality.

I was just pulling the Velcro tight on my sneakers when Mellisande and the rest of her entourage arrived to inspect the troops. The dragon lady looked like she was on her way to some kind of shi shi event where people sip champagne out of cut crystal. She had on a skirt made up of about a hundred sheer handkerchiefs, and a ruby-red sequined blouse to go with. Her shoes came to a wicked point. If only looks could kill…

Everyone kind of stopped what they were doing to straighten and watch her, as she watched us.

"Tonight is the night," Melli announced, pitching her voice to carry. It bounced around the basement like a prize-machine rubber ball. "All of your training, all of our plans, have come down to this. We're going up against the council and we *will* win. I will be going in first with a select few to clear your way. Your job is to come in and clean up any opposition. Once we hold the council, we hold the region and from there … anything is possible. We will make our own rules, take what we want, feed where and when we will."

It sounded like she was running for student body president. Power hummed out of her as if she were trying to affect all her peeps at once, but it was like a fine drizzle, not gonna do more than maybe whet their appetites—not like Bobby's tidal wave of power.

"Are you with me?" she asked.

There was a general cheer of agreement, but I didn't think it was all she could have hoped for.

Her eyes narrowed as her gaze swept the room. "Good. The alternative is unthinkable."

I looked around at the others. They definitely wanted to hurt something, but I wasn't so sure it was Mellisande's enemies.

She swept out of the room with her skirt flowing behind her, leaving two of her entourage behind—Connor and Larry, weirdly, the oldest and newest of her inner circle.

Connor studied the faces around him, his gaze meeting mine for just a second before moving on, but it seemed like he was doing that a lot. Making visual contact with his team, maybe.

"Team Alpha, to me," he said, confirming it. He moved off to one side, leaving the other half of the room to Larry, who called out, "Team Beta."

Trevor and Cassandra, who'd become the inseparables, actually split in order to flank me in the line-up.

"Melli's going out the front with her entourage, to draw any watchers away with her," Trevor whispered.

I'd filled him in last night in the wee hours before dawn along with a few select others. I wished there'd been more I could trust, but who—Chaz and Tina? Larry's new flirtation, book-girl?

"How do you know that?" I whispered back.

"Look at how she's dressed. She wants them to think she's going there to party, not to provoke. She's hoping to put them off guard. It's what I'd do. Minus the skirt, of course."

I bit my lip to keep from pointing out that he didn't protest the sparkly shirt, but sobered as Connor's gaze swept over us again. As soon as he'd moved on, I asked, "What about *him*?" I jerked my head in Connor's direction. "Won't the council expect him to be with her?"

Trevor gave that a moment of thought. "Probably she could say she left him behind to hold down the fort, if it comes to that."

"Something you want to share?" Connor asked, glaring right at us.

"Sir, no sir," Trevor said, stiffening to attention. It was totally tin soldier … and yet maybe just a little hot, like I could almost visualize him in uniform. Not that I'd admit it out loud. Besides, I had prophecy boy, and that totally trumped soldier boy any day of the week.

Connor looked to me. "No," I spat. "Nothing to share."

"Good, then listen up."

We were going out the tunnel—no surprise there. Then we were going to divide and conquer. Team Alpha one way, Beta the other. Follow directions. That was all we needed to know. That, and "this is not a game. This is the real thing, boys and girls. Your weapons are locked and loaded. Holy water, real wooden stakes and arrows. Don't shoot yourselves in the foot. Don't shoot each other. This video game doesn't have a restart button. Got it?"

Some of the guys looked like this was wicked cool, but most looked like they could have grasped the concept of *not a game* without Connor trying to meet us at our supposed level with the video game references.

"I'll cover you," Trevor whispered, risking Connor's wrath. Obviously he'd noticed my serious lack of combat skills.

"Thanks," I whispered back.

Connor motioned for Team Beta to proceed us, and I watched Pam and Vanessa, Larry's new flirtation, the girls whose hair I'd styled, and others file past me. My chest tightened, and I felt strangely like a mama bear watching my cubs march off to war—which didn't even make sense.

Even best-case scenario, some of those kids wouldn't be coming back. I just couldn't imagine that the lot of us, with only a few weeks of training, were going to take down a seasoned council—who I'd imagine had lookouts and enforcers and the whole bit . . . even if we did have an inside man and a psychic cyclone who could be unleashed.

Connor waited for Beta to get some distance on us and approached the hatch himself. I was expecting he would lead the charge, but instead he rapped out the code to close it up.

Trevor and I exchanged a look.

"Are we going out the front?" I asked, thinking that just maybe Trevor was right and Melli'd drawn off the watchers, making it safe for us to take another route to the council house—which presumably we'd come at from different directions anyway, to kind of surround them.

He gave me a wintry glare. "No."

A chill ran right up my spine, and out to all points until my fingers nearly tingled in shock.

"You're leaving them hanging," I guessed. "It'll be a bloodbath."

His lips pulled back from his teeth, and I could see the points, deadly and glistening like a snake about to strike. Was that what I looked like when I fed? Ew, maybe it was a good thing we didn't show up in mirrors.

"It'll be a bloodbath anyway," he hissed. "I'm saving you. When it's all over, we'll come to our own understanding with the council. We will live."

I looked at the others. Unlike their lack of reaction to the human-shaped archery targets, there was real horror in their eyes now. Connor might be old enough to have lost his humanity, but we were still young. We remembered. I didn't see selling my soul, assuming I still had one, as "saving" myself.

I looked around, waiting for someone to speak up. I was surprised when it was me.

"Listen up, people!" I said, raising my voice loud enough to carry. "Do we want to be led by a loser who would sacrifice our friends and tell us it's for our own good?"

There were a few murmurs of "no," Trevor and Cassandra the loudest.

"Are you all ready to kick some butt? If we fight for ourselves, for our friends, we can do *anything*. Remember Marcy and Rick. Think of Bobby. Connor is willing to sacrifice us all just the way Mellisande did. I say NO MORE!"

There was a roar of agreement this time. People were getting over their shock, getting psyched for battle. Staying behind was like pulling an all-nighter only to find out the test was cancelled. We were prepped and ready. I almost had *myself* convinced I wasn't sending everyone into sudden death.

"Grab him!" I ordered, sweeping a hand and pointing a finger right at Connor.

The group surged forward before Connor even had time to pull together a decent whammy. The first guy to reach for him froze halfway there, looking shocked as his grasping hands fell to his sides, but Connor could only mentally reach one of us at a time, and within seconds he was overwhelmed.

"Bring him," I said. "He knows the plan. He knows where we're headed."

"And if he won't tell us?" Trevor asked, holding tight to one of Connor's arms.

"I'll leave that to you." I didn't even know what I meant by that—I didn't think ROTC trained their guys in interrogation and torture. I hoped not anyway. But Trevor nodded like it was something he could handle, and I breathed a sigh of relief.

"Let's move out!" I ordered.

I played my little tune on the door and it opened before us. I could totally get used to this being taken seriously and being, like, the Pied Piper of vamps, if only I weren't so freaked that I was leading us into war. I still didn't know exactly what had possessed me or what we'd find at the council place. I didn't know the layout or the other troop movements or whatever. I didn't know how many we were up against. What the hell was I doing?

Team Beta had left the weapons locker open assuming we'd be right behind them, and I ordered everyone to load up. It was kind of a heady feeling to be obeyed.

For myself, I grabbed about five water guns and loaded them from the bottle of holy water Trevor passed to me, very, very careful not to get any on myself, and more care-

170

ful not to consider what the effects meant for my soul. I mean, I wasn't using it for anything, but still...

Trevor's weapons of choice were the guns and the pointy stakes—the real wood kind and not our little practice points. Bows and arrows would be way too bulky once the enemy got close enough to see the whites of our eye-teeth. He also found a load of the zip-tie cuffs Melli's minions had used on Bobby and me when they kidnapped us. He promptly put them to use on Connor, who snarled and kicked and flailed and generally made a nuisance of himself until Trevor shot him in the chest with a blast of holy water. It ate right through his shirt and started in on his flesh, with a smell of burnt hair and boiled blood that I did my best to ignore, along with his outraged howl.

I thought about the news report I'd seen, where Bobby was wanted for questioning and all. Maybe if I tipped off the police, they'd put a stop to the violence. It wasn't like they could lock Bobby up once they realized the bodies he was accused of snatching were walking around under their own steam. But I'd be sending regular humans up against vamps, totally unprepared. And, if they lived through it, we vamps would be exposed—incite a national panic, maybe, or be used as lab rats.

No, there wasn't anyone I could call in for reinforcements. We were on our own.

Cassandra jogged up next to me and asked quietly, "You have a plan?"

"I'm open to suggestions," I told her.

"That would be 'no'?"

"I'm working on it."

"Work faster," she suggested.

"Great, thanks."

As we exited the tunnel, I aimed my own water gun at Connor. "Our ride is in the school parking lot?"

He looked like he was doing his very best to shoot daggers out of his eyes, but failing miserably. "Yes," he answered through clenched teeth.

I led the way, trying to march tall despite my uncomfortable height deprivation. I was totally confident in my three-inch heels, but take those away...at least my new kicks didn't sink into the ground, 'cause it had totally rained during the day. My sneaks were wet by the time we reached the van in the lot. It was the same one Bobby and I had seen that first day, a lifetime ago, idling outside the sporting goods store while Chickzilla, Rick, and Larry raided it.

"Who has their license?" I asked, not even sure why I was worried about that. We had way bigger problems than a ticket if the police stopped us and recognized anyone.

"I do," half the kids chimed. I chose a spiky-haired guy who just looked like the speed-demon type, figuring if we needed any quick getaways...

"You, what's your name?"

"Frank."

"Good. Frank, you're in the hot seat."

Trevor frisked Connor for the keys and tossed them to

Frank, who got a huge grin on his face like he'd just found his happy place.

I didn't even have to tell anyone what to do next. As soon as Frank had the doors open, I called shotgun and the rest piled in.

"Where to?" Trevor asked, and I craned my neck to see what kind of threat he was using on Connor now. In close quarters he'd chosen the stake, rather than risk incidental damage with the water pistol. He was holding it just south of where I figured Connor's heart would be.

"Turn right out of the lot," Connor answered unhappily, but his eyes seemed kind of vacant. Either he'd given up or he was busy plotting.

Frank gunned the van and it lurched forward, knocking everyone back. Just as we were pulling out of the lot a car flew out of nowhere to cut us off. Frank slammed the brakes instead of the gas this time, throwing us all forward again into whiplash territory. But it wasn't soon enough to avoid a head-on collision with the broadside of a car I knew way too well, and a driver who the others thought dead. They'd witnessed his execution, after all.

"Damn it. Rick!" I yelled, like he could hear me through the van window.

Rick nearly fell out of his car, staggering a step before bracing himself and his very serious crossbow on our hood, the bolt aimed right toward our driver. His eyes were a mile wide, but I couldn't tell if it was sheer adrenaline or something to do with Connor and mind control.

"You're not going anywhere." Connor spoke for him, solving that mystery.

"Really, how do you expect to lead when no one else will follow?" I asked reasonably.

"I'll find a way."

"Everybody out of the van," Rick ordered a second later. His voice was raised, but it was also dead flat, like he was speaking someone else's … Connor's … words.

"Shoot him," I told Trevor. I could have shot Connor myself, but I figured if he suddenly had to control Trevor, he'd lose control over Rick and I'd have a chance to get through to him.

I wasn't counting on Connor turning Trevor's hand against himself. "Cass, help him!" I cried, "Cassandra" being way too long to spit out in an emergency.

She lunged for the gun and a crossbow bolt pierced the windshield just to my left, halfway between me and Frank, who let lose a "Holy shit!"

I jumped nearly out of my skin and whirled on Rick, who was staring through the windshield.

"Rick!" I yelled, fixing on his anime-huge eyes. "Change sides and I'll turn you, right freakin' now! No more games, no more feeling your body dying around you, just eternal life."

Rick's crossbow twitched and Frank pulled his own bow and arrow, like it would really go through glass. Rick's bolt had to have been steel-tipped—not to mention that his crossbow looked way tougher than Frank's more traditional bow.

"Down, boy," I told Frank. "Rick?"

There was another tense second of silence, during which I looked back to see that Cassandra had won the battle for Trevor's gun and Connor now had way too many muzzles pointing at him to control them all. They were only water guns—some brightly colored and all completely plastic—but there was no mistaking they meant business. Connor's control faltered.

"Gina?" Rick called out. "I'm in. I'll lower my weapon, but only if you come out alone."

I swallowed a breath in order to heave a sigh of relief. It could be a trick, but every second of our stand-off was another one in which our friends in Team Beta went without backup. I had to risk it.

"You," I said, making eye contact with Trevor and Cass, "find out where we're headed. Beat it out of Connor if you have to. You," I said to Frank, "*drive*." To everyone else, "Follow Trevor's orders. Win the day! I'm taking alternate transport." I waved a hand at Rick's T-bird.

"But I don't know—" Trevor protested.

"And I do?"

That shut him up. I opened the van door and descended into the face of a bolt pointed just slightly away from me. It was clear it could swing around at any moment.

I slapped the side of the van twice like it was a reluctant horse, and Frank put it into reverse to pull a hasty turn.

I only hoped everyone got to the council house in one piece.

"Well?" Rick challenged, eying me warily, like *I* might be the trickster.

"Give me your wrist," I said impatiently, because there was no way I was necking with the rat, even to save us both.

"You just want me to take my hand off the weapon."

"Duh. What choice do you have? You think you'll be in a position to shoot me if we're neck and neck?"

He got one of those wicked guy smiles on his face. "We could find out."

"Ewww. Pass. Now, *the wrist*."

Nervously, Rick took a hand off his crossbow and offered it to me. His nails were in worse shape than mine, bitten to the quick and bumpy besides, like he wasn't eating right. I was totally glad I had the vamp immunity and couldn't get rabies or scabies or anything from him.

"Ready?" I asked.

He nodded, but then winced as I bit in, his hand jerking just a bit. I held firm and he subsided, even moaning like it was good for him. It icked me out enough that I didn't get carried away. A little was more than enough. My hunger wasn't too certain of that though, and I used my still-elongated teeth to open a nick in my own wrist.

Rick's eyes looked dazed. He lost his grip on the crossbow with the unbitten hand and didn't even notice when it fell to the ground.

"Suck," I offered, holding my arm out.

He swayed, as if maybe I'd taken too much and he was going to pass out. I slapped him and it felt so good I did it again on the other cheek. He snapped out of it with a glare.

"Your turn to drink," I told him.

A look of *ugh* crossed his face, and then he bent his head to lick at the blood welling on my wrist.

"Ick. Suck or don't suck, but don't lap at it like a dog."

Rick grabbed my wrist to keep me from pulling back and sucked like a Hoover.

I yanked it away when I was sure he had enough.

"Okay, let's roll," I said, yanking open the passenger door to the T-bird.

"But I don't feel any different!"

"Don't make me 'duh' you again. Really. You're still alive, like a pre-vamp or something. If you're lucky you'll die tonight. I may kill you myself. Now, let's *go*."

20

Gina! a voice called in my head.

"Bobby!" I answered out loud.

"What?" Rick asked, swerving just a little as his gaze strayed from the road.

"Never mind, just keep driving. And step on it. We're already behind!"

He looked at me like I'd lost it, but I was totally getting used to that.

Bobby? I asked, in my head this time.

Where are you? It was almost like we had a bad connection or someone was sitting on the volume control of a remote, the way the sound wobbled.

On the way.

Better hurry!

Have the reinforcements arrived?

They—he cut out on me, and I banged both hands down on the dashboard. I looked over at the speedometer, which only said 75. I was pretty sure this thing could go faster than that.

"Is this what 'step on it' means to you?"

"The T-bird isn't exactly new. It starts to shake itself apart at 80."

I threw a leg over the junk between us and stamped down on his foot. The car jumped forward, more like a bronco than a bird, and true to Rick's words felt like an earthquake on wheels.

"H-h-how f-f-far?" I asked, my teeth clacking together.

"An-n-nother f-f-five," he answered.

It was less than that when we spotted Team Beta's van, abandoned in a ditch just a few feet from a nearly hidden driveway that went up a hill to something that couldn't even be seen from the road. Alpha must have driven straight up to the door.

"The s-surprise is already b-b-b-blown," I said. "N-n-no need to h-hoof it."

He slowed to take the turn, and my liquefied insides thanked him. Trees obscured our view all the way up the hill, reaching nearly to the car, blocking out even the night sky. When we came free of them, the house before us could have been a temple—large and square, with mile-high pillars and a triangular piece below the roof that had some kind of raised design I didn't have time to appreciate. I did notice that not all the figures in the design were clothed ... or even proportional.

The front door hung open on its hinges. An arm blocked it from closing, its fingers curled to the sky like a spider gone belly-up.

"Whoa," Rick said, voice hushed.

"Let's go."

We got out of the car and approached slowly. All was quiet—here at least. The fight had moved on.

There was no body to go with the arm in the entrance, which we had to step over. But there was remarkably little blood, and I did my best to pretend it was some drama club prop, like from *Sweeney Todd*.

Farther in we could hear the fighting—furniture getting knocked around, bodies hitting the wall, *hard*.

"Ladies first," Rick offered, sweeping a hand before him.

"Yeah, 'cause I really want *you* covering my butt."

"It's a dirty job, but someone has to do it."

I couldn't waste any more time trading mediocre banter with Rick-the-rat. I only hoped I'd have a lifetime to do denial on the idea that he was now my offspring or whatever it's called in the vamp world. I so wasn't ready for motherhood. I could only imagine the Popsicle-stick art I'd get for mother's day. And it made his smarmy comments that much grosser.

Bobby! I called out mentally, hoping I'd get a fix on him and the center of the action, but I got nothing. Again I clung to the thought that he was just occupied elsewhere, and not dead.

It was all fun and games—blood trails, the occasional body part or hank of hair ripped out by the roots, in one case a shoe with a broken heel—until we hit the staircase into the unknown. Unknown because blocking the sight of what lay beyond was Team Alpha, Trevor at the head, slashing about him with a sharpened stake. The others weren't doing as well. Weapons had been dropped, making the stairs treacherous. Already I could see teammates who had fallen fighting the council vamps. My heart did its best to climb into my throat.

Trevor himself went down with no warning whatsoever, like someone had just grabbed his feet out from under him. He held onto the stake and it flailed dangerously at everyone within range. Without thinking, I vaulted over Trevor's downed body, ready to stand between him and his rival, when something else pounced, knocking Trevor's opponent to the floor. Suddenly, I was face-to-face with a pair of fiery red eyes. The psychic crouched, smiling at me with gleaming, blood-stained teeth. The freakshow had clearly fed recently. I hoped for Trevor's sake that he was full.

From below, a girl blasted the boogeyman with a stream of holy water, and the freak did nothing but turn its head, totally unnaturally, like an owl or Linda Blair spitting pea soup. He focused on the girl and spasmed strangely, like he was about to hoc a loogey. Then, without warning, he spit out a stream of blood that must have been mixed with something stronger than stomach acid, the way the girl screamed … and screamed … and screamed.

My brain shrieked at me to run, but it didn't seem like we were on speaking terms because, for some stupid reason, I totally ignored it.

"Get. Off. Him," I ordered.

"Make me," he hissed.

And me fresh out of hair spray and lanterns.

"It's not us you want."

"Don't tell me what I want," he roared.

"Okay, fine. I've pissed you off. You want a piece of me, I get that. But now? With all these distractions? Don't you want to take your time? Like, pair me with a nice Chianti?"

I was now officially over that *have you lost your mind* look.

"Are you using *logic?*" he snarled.

I ignored Rick's snicker and focused my glare.

"What, like I'm incapable because I'm a girl?"

"No, because you're *you.*"

I wanted my super power to be fire-breathing. I'd roast him where he crouched.

"Fine, come and get me." I pretended he was a downed log between me and the only mochachino machine on a deserted island and literally took a run at him, avoiding his snapping teeth and throwing him off balance by planting two fists on his back so I could vault over him. My gym teacher would have been so proud, once she woke out of her dead faint.

I tried not to look back, knowing I'd be faster if I didn't, but something compelled me. I turned to see that the freakshow had unfurled his legs again and seemed to be leaping on all fours, more like a grasshopper or monkey than a man-like thing. There was no sanity in those eyes whatsoever. I put on a burst of speed that had to come from total terror, following the path of the fallen, hurdling over things I didn't even want to think about. There was a horrible clatter behind me and I figured the freakshow had gotten tangled in one of the bowstrings or something, but I didn't look back again.

Bobby! I screamed in my head.

Here. It was faint, like there was a barrier, but it was unmistakably ahead. It seemed weird that I could tell direction from a word, but life had gone so far off the normal track into bizarro-world that I didn't even expect things to make sense anymore.

"This way!" I yelled to Rick, in case he couldn't just track the trail of the great galloping ghastly behind me. I hoped he and the others were close behind.

The scene I burst in on stopped me cold, and let the freakshow knock me ass-over-ankles in a flying tackle. We rolled across the floor, my spine snapping and twisting over bodies, but not nearly so many as I'd feared. We were moving too quickly to see if the bodies belonged to anyone I knew, and one girl in a tracksuit was missing the better part of her face anyway. Denial reared its blessed head, and my thoughts shut down. We were vamps. We could regrow faces, right? That was as far as I got. The Crypt Keeper wound up on top, with me pinned painfully over something extremely pointy. From the way my body shivered violently at the contact, that thing was wooden and probably stake-shaped.

But now that I was under control, the freakshow wasn't paying any attention to me. He was looking around the room, eyes focusing like lasers on Mellisande, who stood—torn, bloody, hair half in her face—with most of her cabal and what was left of Team Beta, in a face-off with the council. We must have reached the inner sanctum.

The council and the minions had retreated behind some forcefield thing my boyfriend was straining to hold. Sweat poured down Bobby's face, red like blood, and his hair was in his gorgeous eyes. He was the most beautiful thing I'd ever seen. Not that I'd ever tell him. Guys got weird about things like that. But I was so totally proud of him, holding a barrier against outright bloodshed.

He met my eyes as I lay there pinned and mouthed something that looked like *I love you*, and I went all stupid girly gooey inside. I stiffened against the feeling, that mellow lose-yourself-in-someone-else ... thing ... and a tiny shift away from the stake helped just a little with the shaking. And, see, if I'd melted I'd have been a goner. Love was poison. Too bad it came in such a cute package.

"Bobby, drop the shield," Mellisande ordered, ignoring the psycho-psychic and our little interruption. My posse, Team Alpha, crowded in through the doorway behind me, stopping cold to assess the scene.

"No," Bobby grated out. "Didn't open the doors. Won't help you kill."

So he'd resisted whatever compulsion she'd put on him to aid her invasion. Go him! But it was clear he couldn't hold out forever. More blood was going to be shed. Probably even his.

"Lemurs!" I yelled. It was our school identity. I only hoped enough people had the spirit. "Are we going to let these vamps throw us into their stupid war or are we going to fight for ourselves?" I called out.

"Ourselves!" Bobby yelled from behind the barrier, backing me up. Mellisande glared daggers at him.

The psychic focused his freaky eyes back on me... or really, *un*-focused back on me. His face was looking my way but his gaze was totally elsewhere, like he was trying to see the future.

"Do you *mind?*" I asked.

I don't know what he saw, but slowly he pulled his body off mine. I didn't trust it.

"Alistaire!" Mellisande shrieked.

The council bastard and babe from Melli's study gasped at the name. "It can't be," the man said.

"He doesn't even look—" the woman breathed.

"Human?" Alistaire asked, laughing that creepy-crawly laugh of his. "No, pretty pretty, I don't expect I do. Alistaire has left the building."

"But you're dead," the man hissed. "Mellisande killed you."

"Indeed she did," the psycho—Alistaire—admitted. "I am death itself. Death warmed over. The angel of death. Yes, that's it. I am the dark angel of death that creeps upon his petty pace."

If a vampire could pale, the councilman did. I didn't know what the heck Alistaire was talking about, but clearly it meant more to him than it did to me. Who was this Alistaire that his resurrection rocked their world? But then it came to me. Hadn't the council people practically accused Melli of killing her sire? Could he be…? But how? Had she tried and failed to kill him, somehow turning him into the twisted thing he was today? Maybe they'd even concocted a scheme together to release Alistaire from the council's control, and it had gone horribly wrong.

But whatever the past, right now was the perfect opportunity for us to strike, while everyone was still reeling.

"Now!" I shouted, rising to my feet and grabbing the lone water pistol still lodged in my pants, becoming one with my ribs.

The remains of Alpha and Beta teams rose up.

Melli spun, trying to face down all angles of threat. Her remaining minions—the Chick, Hawkman, Things

One and Two, blond-lady-without-nickname, Sparky—all closed around her like some kind of panty shield.

But *my* minions, my Lemurs, my ... *friends* closed around them, greater in number and all righteously pissed at seeing their buds go down in the dragon lady's play for power.

And then all hell broke loose. The first shot was fired, and a woman's high-pitched shriek split my eardrums. But I couldn't see which side it was coming from, because Bobby's power had just given out and he and the shield both went down.

I launched myself toward him and the council lady intercepted me. I held her at water-gun-point while she had only her fangs and killer nails filed to points. Nice manicure, though—a little faux diamond chip on each tip.

"He's mine," I told her.

"Ours," the lady hissed.

I shot her right between the eyes and body-checked her to the ground as she howled in pain, so that I could stand between Bobby and the world—which was totally lame, since *he* had all the power.

The wench recovered almost instantly and grabbed me by the arm, her diamond tips digging into me like spikes. She whirled me around, away from Bobby and back toward the chaos that had erupted around us. I lifted the water gun to fire again, but my hand knocked into someone with an impact that hit a nerve or something, 'cause my hand went numb and flew open. The gun went end over end, striking

Chickzilla with the butt, but to no effect. I, meanwhile, was getting my arm nearly yanked from the socket. My ankle twisted as I tried to wrench myself away, and I fell halfway to the ground with my arm still behind me and up at a really awkward angle. Around me were *ki-yahs* and other sounds of power, snarls and growls of rage. In battle, no one could hear me whimper—I took full advantage of that.

Until something grabbed my other arm and jerked me away from my captor—or tried to. For a second I felt like I was being drawn and quartered, like Mel Gibson in *Braveheart* (when he was still cuter than he was crazy). I couldn't suck in a breath to howl. My vision started to spot. And then something gave. For a second I thought it was me, that my body had snapped and the lack of pain was death, but the backlash of sudden release flung me into the thing that had used me as the rope in his tug of war.

Hawkman.

"It isn't enough that you've killed me once?" I asked, my chest aching with the effort to push air through it.

He didn't answer, just kept swinging me, right into the arms of my nemesis—Melli-noma. Then he turned to deal with the council chick himself.

"You are so dead," Melli told me.

"Well, duh. Thanks for the news flash."

I might not have said it if I'd noticed the stake in her hand. I had nothing. No more water guns, no pointy sticks. I was a goner.

188

Mellisande lunged at me, her stick poised to kill, and I had nowhere to go. Not with Hawkman fighting a hairsbreadth away and leaving me no room at all, except maybe for a fateful trip. I didn't even get that lucky. The point pierced me like butter. The flare of pain was so intense my vision went black, my knees buckled, and I slid to the ground. But I was not dead. Smelly Melli's aim, like her personality, was off. Still, there was nothing I could do if she gave it another try. Nothing about my body was obeying me. I willed my hands to reach for the stake, to turn it on Melli, but every, like, synapse or whatever in my brain was flooded with *ack, there's a freakin' stick poking out of my chest* messages.

Someone hit Mellisande, and she nearly went down on top of me before Hawkman leapt to her aid. The action moved on around me, leaving me for dead.

Gina? a voice asked in my head.

Bobby?

Such warmth wrapped around me that I almost forgot all about the stake and the fact that some of these people were here, fighting, hopefully not dying, because of me, *and* that I hadn't seen hide nor hair of Marcy. It was like the sun on the first really warm day of spring, when the whole world comes out in shorts to play catch or Frisbee or whatever. My heart swelled so much I thought it was going to brush up against the stake.

"Enough!" Bobby shouted, no longer in my head. Power reverberated out of him with the force of a rock-show stage amp. It was enough power to goose my goose bumps and bring the hair all over my body to attention, making it very clear how desperately I needed to shave certain parts. Everyone in the room froze, except me. Suddenly I felt as if my hands might almost work again—like Bobby's blast of power had given me a boost. Squeezing my eyes shut with the effort, I lifted hands that felt more like anvils to my chest and struggled to close them around the stake.

Meanwhile, Bobby held the room spellbound.

"There's a new power in town, and it is *us*," he said, sounding totally recovered—strong even. A force to be reckoned with. "I don't care about your struggles, but you will fight them somewhere else. Mozulla is a high school town now!"

The power of his words rushed over me and through the room. It was as if he wasn't just laying down the law, but like he was laying down *reality*—which was way, way cooler. I wondered if either side would have let him live if they'd known he could do this.

I was still tingling when I pulled the stake from my chest ... slowly, because that was all I could manage. My body jerked, but I managed to hang on to the stake and finish the job. It was a good thing I was already on the floor, because the pain would have dropped me where I stood.

"Lemurs, let's move out," Bobby finished.

He came to help me to my feet, and I gasped as he slipped his hands beneath my arms to lift me. My chest was on fire.

"I can't hold them long," he whispered in my ear, totally ruining the *my boyfriend is a demigod* fantasy.

I did the best I could to get my feet under me.

"Marcy?" I whispered back.

"I think I know where they're holding her."

It must have taken titanic strength to hold some people frozen and release others. That had to be why, when I swept the room to see who was still standing, I saw both Mellisande and the psychic twitch. I remembered Connor saying that Melli was resistant, like me. I could only hope that Bobby, as "the key," had grown enough power to hold her. The psychic... well, he was a law unto himself.

The others moved out—Frank, the spiky-haired guy who'd driven the van, Cassandra, Katie and Di, and more. On the ground I spotted a pixie cut and recognized my work. I went to the fallen girl and turned her over. My heart broke. There was nothing I could do. Someone's aim had been better than Melli's.

"Back here," Bobby reminded me, standing at the exit where the other kids had gotten while the getting was good.

I went too, stepping over one more familiar body—Rick's. His chest was still rising and falling, but just barely. It seemed so weird that the pixie girl, an immortal vampire, wouldn't live on while Rick, the human, would. Which meant I had to take him with us. I couldn't leave him for the council.

"Help me," I appealed to Bobby. If I hadn't taken the

chest wound, I probably could have handled Rick myself with my super vamp strength, but as it was my chest felt like it was going to rip in two. I was going to need some serious blood to heal, and my one and only human minion had temporarily checked out.

Bobby helped me drag him into the hall. After we were all through he closed the door and, like, fused it or something. Then he told me I was on my own. It was up to me to drag Rick and lead the others to safety. He'd go for Marcy.

I was about ready to suggest that *he* do the dragging and I do the rescuing when something went BUMP against the closed door.

"Quickly!" he said. And since he knew where he was going on the Marcy-front and I didn't, I suddenly saw the sense in being the one to get out.

We found Trevor lying where he'd fallen on the steps, groaning, his eyes just flickering open.

"Trevor!" I snapped, and his lids shot open, zeroing in on me with only a little drifting. "If you're not going to die today, I need your help. Snap to. Get everyone to the vans."

Cassandra shot me a shocked look and rushed out from behind me to help Trevor stand, but I was counting on duty to drive him, like a good soldier, to get himself and everyone else out alive.

I let the others stream past, holding only Di back to help with my dead-weight issue.

"Ewww," she said when she touched Rick, taking some of his weight. "He's dead."

"Hello! Pot, kettle. Besides, he's only unconscious," I said. "He'll get better."

She didn't argue, but she was as skeeved at touching him as I was at the thought of mayonnaise or cottage cheese. Particularly cottage cheese. I shuddered. Nothing should look like that. Certainly nothing that went into my body.

"Get to the vans," I shouted out. "Fill one up—and go! Leave one for the rest of us."

Though if I had my way, I'd be taking the T-bird myself. That was a sweet ride.

We hit a traffic jam when the leaders of our group stopped to pick up another downed friend, the owner of the arm blocking the front door. From the looks of her, she was miraculously still living, although none too happy about it at that moment. And then we were off again. Behind us, the banging against the door began in earnest, and I knew that Bobby's whammy had worn off.

"Come on, come on, come on," I chanted under my breath, thinking of Bobby and Marcy and how they were *not allowed* to get themselves captured again. And true death was absolutely out.

We broke from the house into the dark of night and made a mad dash for the van in the driveway.

"Go, go, go!" I encouraged, though no one seemed to need it.

Everyone piled in, even though there were way more

people than seats, but someone—Trevor?—solved some of the space issues by opening the back doors and throwing Connor out on his ass. I wondered how Connor would explain himself to Melli when she got free (if the council didn't finish her off), but I didn't really care. But even with the extra room, there was no place for Rick and me in the van.

"Cram in," I told Di. "I'll take him from here."

She eased Rick's weight back fully onto me and did as I said.

"Get back to Mellisande's place," I shouted through the open van door. "Start thinking of ways to secure it in case they come after us."

"Who died and made you boss," someone yelled, clearly a remnant of Team Beta, 'cause Alpha and I had already worked these things out.

"No one. *Yet*," I answered.

It was enough for now. We could be all democratic tomorrow. Tonight I didn't think I was asking too much.

Frank was already set up in the driver's seat. He reached over to all but slam the van door in my face and took off with a squeal of tires. I didn't have to tell him twice to get the hell out of dodge. I jumped back as he missed my toes by a whisper. I wanted to curse him, but he was only following orders and if I really was "chaos" (which I doubted), I didn't want to doom the whole van to a head-on collision due to his being a jerk.

I turned my energies to a quick frisk of Rick for his

keys. I couldn't help thinking he'd be sorry he missed that. The keys were in his right pocket and he dressed left, so, thankfully, I missed out on a really awkward moment.

I got us to the T-bird, contorted myself and Rick until I was able to lay him across the back seat, and got into the driver's side. Then I waited. I'd told myself I wouldn't, that there was the other van for Bobby and Marcy. But I didn't think Bobby knew how to hotwire a vehicle—not with his whole white-knight upbringing. Plus, it just felt wrong to go off without them, like I was turning my back.

If it hadn't been for Rick, I probably would have rushed back in. But without cell phones or anything (note to self: when *I* run things, we all get touch screens), we'd be playing a game of Marco Polo to find each other, and that would only slow things down, maybe long enough for the council to break down that door.

So I waited. It couldn't have been as long as it seemed ... so long that I died of boredom five times over ... and then finally Bobby and Marcy came stumbling out. She looked like heck—like someone had tried to give her a G.I. Jane cut in front and left the back long. It was like the worst mullet ever, but at least the scalp was growing back.

I tumbled out of the driver's seat and we hugged. Marcy cried great sloppy tears that I knew would stain red, so it was a good thing I was wearing dark colors.

"Can we do this later?" Bobby asked, looking behind him.

There was an explosion from inside the house, much

like a door bursting outward and slamming against the opposite wall. Marcy screamed.

"Get in the back," I told her, practically pushing her in on top of Rick.

She screamed again as Bobby and I got into the front. I'd left the car running, and now I floored it. Pedal all the way to the metal. The T-bird leapt forward, kicking up gravel, and we were off.

Bobby craned his neck to look back, apparently not trusting the rearview mirror.

"Are they following?" I asked.

"No." He sounded surprised.

"Why not?" It was a stupid question, like I *wanted* them to follow, but it just popped out.

"If I had to guess—not enough time left in the night for another battle. They have no plans, not even a head-count of who they've got standing. Plus, they've still got to deal with Mellisande and her people."

"But tomorrow?"

"Maybe. We're new at this, but if I were the council, I wouldn't give us time to figure out what we're doing."

"You don't think your whammy will hold?"

"Is that what we're calling it these days?"

I gave him a cheeky smile. "You have a better word?"

He smiled back at me, and for a minute I forgot what we were talking about. It was totally killer to have him to myself again.

"Watch out for that tree!" Marcy yelled from the back.

I'd been drifting over to the side of the road, which on the outskirts of Mozulla either meant guard rails or trees. I yanked the car back toward center. The spell was broken.

"You okay?" I asked her finally. Bad friend, no cookie.

She looked at me in disbelief from her perch atop Rick's legs. "Sure. J. Lo wig and a shower, I'll be good as new."

"That's my girl."

"So, you in charge now?" she asked.

I looked at Bobby. "Partially, I guess."

"Wicked."

21

So here we were, a whole houseful of vamps with no human minions to guard us when we fell into a dead, vulnerable sleep for the day. Our enemies, whether Melli or the council, weren't so handicapped ... and Melli's people had a key and passcodes.

Since Bobby had been separated out and hadn't lived with everyone the way I had, it was to me—*me*—that everyone looked to for a defense strategy. It was totally weird. I thought of what I'd do if I was like a queen or a crown princess or a pop diva, and delegated.

"Trev, the basement is yours. You figure out what to do about that trap door and all. When you finish, come back and see about the windows up here."

"Trev?" Cassandra muttered dangerously, like I'd stumbled onto her nickname for him.

"Like I have time for two whole syllables. Go!"

Trevor tagged a couple more kids and headed with Cassandra toward the basement.

"Bobby, any ideas about the front and back doors?"

"Pennies."

"Pennies?" I repeated stupidly.

"Sure, it's an old trick. You jam a mess of pennies between the door and its frame and there's *nothing* getting in or out—unless you bust through the door itself."

I just kind of looked at him. "Um, great. Except we don't know where Melli keeps her change jar. Maybe you can seal the doors like you did back at the council compound?"

"We saw how well that worked," he answered. "I think I'd better save my strength."

"Right." I thought for a second, then fell back on a classic. "Okay, gang, we're doing an old-fashioned barricade. If it moves, I want it in front of doors and windows."

It would have been so much easier to just string garlic and crosses up in the windows, but it was kind of hard to fight an enemy when you had the same weaknesses. Anyway,

I kinda doubted somehow that Melli kept a supply of religious stuff on hand.

"Chop chop!" I said, realizing everyone was still looking at me. "Double time." They flew into a flurry of activity.

I grabbed Bobby as he was about to run off. This power thing was kind of *wow*, but if anything went wrong it would be totally my fault.

"What am I forgetting?" I asked him.

His eyes were shining. Some guys would have been royally pissed at taking directions from a girl, but not mine. "I think you're doing great."

"Well, snap out of it," I said. "I need you to be totally critical. Lay it on me."

He thought about it, eyes on my lips like ideas weren't the only things he was thinking of laying on me. I let myself imagine a moment of peace and a private room for all of one second. "Later," I told him, my voice gone all strangely husky.

"Promise?" he asked.

"If it's in my power. Now, how do we keep the peace?"

"Peace I don't know about, but sanctuary … The windows are too vulnerable. Even if we could find enough junk to pile up to them, it would be precarious, easily toppled. Besides, defense isn't going to win this. Much as I hate to say it, we need to go on the offensive." He bit the lip that *I* wanted to be biting. Well, nipping anyway. "I've got it. A punji stake pit!"

"A what?"

"It's like a prehistoric hunting technique. Drive prey toward a pit lined with stakes, and the butchering is done for you."

I shuddered. "So we should dig pits under the windows and let our enemies fall in?"

"No, no, no." He waved his hands around to banish that image. "We nail the stakes into the window panes on all sides, pointed toward center, and do what we can to angle them outward so that anyone coming through the windows is, if not impaled, at least seriously shredded by the spikes."

I scrunched up my face in horror, imagining bursting victoriously through a window only to get impaled on a pointy stick. My chest ached just thinking about it. But I had to protect my peeps. Misguided as it was, they were looking to me.

"Do it," I told him, steeling my spine.

"I love it when you're bossy," he said, licking those killer kips.

"And I love it when you go all Alpha male." The *L* word was hard to get out, but at least I wasn't saying "I love you," three little words that mean "now that you've got me, you can start taking me for granted." That was not a road I wanted to walk. Not even in Ferragamos.

"Now go!" I ordered, since he liked it so much. "We're burning moonlight."

He gave me a quick hard kiss that spiked my temperature, and was off.

I went to help the others wrestle Melli's desk to the front door. It occurred to me only as we were getting it into place that by sealing our entrances, we were also cutting off any exits. If trouble came calling, there would be no option for retreat.

22

It was totally luxurious to wake up in a room that didn't hold thirty-plus other kids, and to stretch out and encounter the semi-warm body next to me. Bobby and I had collapsed with the dawn into a bed upstairs, although we hadn't had any time to take advantage of it.

I lifted myself up on my elbow, and watched his eyes flicker open as my hand made contact with his ribs and stroked—there'd just been time for us to strip down to our skivvies, out of our action-marred clothes. I'd almost been hoping that Bobby went commando, but he was a boxers kind of guy. I was down to my Victoria's Secret bikini briefs and demi-cup. A blazing hot smile spread across Bobby's face when he saw me.

"Hey there, gorgeous," he said, voice all husky with sleep.

"Hey yourself, stud."

"I could get used to waking up like this."

In that moment he was just so breathtaking that I forgot to guard myself. "Yeah."

We spent another second on the smoldering look, to build up the tension, and then his lips locked with mine. One of his hands came up to caress my hair and lower my head down onto my pillow so that he hovered above me, supported on one arm. The blood that hadn't wept out of my chest yesterday rushed around my body, putting it on high alert. Better than a mochachino any day, even with a fudge brownie chaser.

Then the hand stroking my hair gently slid down my neck and rested just above the lace of my bra to stroke my chest in a way that was far too respectful for my racing hormones.

A really distant part of me was trying to get my attention—something about not being out of danger yet and needing to be on guard, but far more immediate sensations were demanding my attention.

I slid a hand down Bobby's back and teased my finger along the edge of his boxers, just to taunt him the way he was taunting me. He moaned and pulled back, which was *so* not the desired effect.

"We need to get up," he said, looking deeply into my eyes so that I could see his reluctance. "I don't think Melli or the council will let things go. They may even team up."

"Well, I'm so glad one of us is in control of himself," I answered, a little bitterly. I felt like I'd lost an important battle. I wasn't enough to make him lose his control, and yet I'd been willing to surrender mine. I had to be way, way more careful with myself.

His arms caged me as I tried to roll away to pull some clothes on, and he waited until I looked at him. "I'm saying that I don't want any distractions when I get you alone." He kissed my locked jaw. "Because you're worthy of my full attention." He kissed my eyelids, and it didn't seem remotely brotherly the way he did it. I softened just a bit.

"Fine. But they can't launch an attack *this* quickly. You're going to regret it if this turns out to be our only quiet moment."

"I already do," he said, giving me his most sincere look. Lord help me, I believed him.

"Okay, *fine*. Let's get organized."

"That's the second *fine*. I really am in the doghouse, aren't I? I'll make it up to you."

I looked him in the eye. "Damn straight."

He smirked and my stupid lips betrayed me by creeping

upwards as well. We shared a moment, almost as nice if not as intense as the one earlier.

"Now, get off me so I can get dressed," I ordered, ruining it.

"Yes, ma'am."

"You'd better take a mental picture of me in my skivvies, because if you call me ma'am again, this'll be the last time you see them."

He just grinned at me. I stuck my tongue out and rolled away, too full of confusing emotions to look at him any longer. If only he'd get mad when I said things like that, this whole situation would be a lot easier. But when I pushed, he *smiled*. Threw me off my game.

Whatever. I had an entire closet to explore, and for the first time since I'd been vamped, I could meet my fate in style. The closet, I discovered, belonged to the blond vampire chick, which meant the room was hers as well. Of course, as she was totally a spring and I was totally a summer, the outfit options were limited, but I managed to find a wine-red dress and cute but sturdy wedges to go with it.

I took a quick moment to brush, fluff, and smooth before making an appearance out in the hall, which was already a flurry of activity. It seemed a lot of other kids had also fled the barracks, in favor of the private rooms on the second floor.

Cassandra practically jumped me as I emerged, which was a shock because I thought she'd be cuddled up with

Trevor. "Tammy, the girl whose arm is ... well, she's in a bad way. We need to get her some blood soon. Even so, I don't know—"

"What about the store they keep in the bunker?"

"We checked there last night. All out."

"And the kitchen?"

"A few bottles. Not enough to go around. Either Mellisande was due a shipment or she's got a secret stash somewhere."

I suddenly felt badly about the couple of minutes spent fooling around with Bobby while the others were being all practical. I tried to think what to do. Melli would have said screw the ones who can't fight and strengthen the others—which made my decision a piece of cake.

"Anybody else in Tammy's state?"

"Not that I know of. No one who made it back with us."

There was a moment of silence at that.

"Give her a full bottle. Count how many people we have with us and divide the rest into cups, equal shares. Have Trevor or someone call everyone together downstairs. We need to get organized!"

She nodded, but then hesitated before moving to reach out a hand and squeeze my arm. "Don't worry, you're doing great."

"And if I screw up?" I asked, letting her see the chink in my armor. *See*, I told myself. *You let Bobby in the door and it blows wide open.*

"We'll let you know," she told me.

"Before or after?"

"Don't worry," she repeated. Then she flitted off before I could ask any more tough questions. Like who really cared exactly when a train leaving Boston at a hundred miles per hour and a train leaving New York an hour later at the same speed would meet in a head-on collision?

Yeah, I had train wrecks on the brain, but we'd come this far and now we had, like, the home-field advantage.

Bobby was right behind me, and I felt him press up against my back and slide an arm around my waist to stroke my belly.

He kissed my shoulder. "I'll help round everybody up. Meet you downstairs?"

I nodded, my heart too full to speak.

I took a deep unneeded breath and went downstairs, checking out the doors and windows I passed. I was sure I was forgetting something.

Morsel.

I cringed, wanting to claw my own eyes out just to get at the cancer spreading through my brain at his touch.

'Ware. They come.

It was the last thing I'd expected from him. "What are you up to? Why tell me?" I asked out loud, making a few kids going by look at me funny, like I'd lost my mind. Just what they wanted in a leader.

If they have you, I don't, he answered. No riddles, no double-speak. It probably meant there wasn't a whole lot of time.

I gave up checking the windows to race down to the dorm, but I threw out one final question as I ran. *What are you?*

He chuckled, and the sharp-tipped cancer of his touch spread throughout my mind. *The only way to cheat death is to embrace it.*

So you're death? I asked.

You are chaos—and from where would chaos descend but death?

Ew ew ew—was he claiming to be some kind of relative, like the crazy uncle in the attic? It was almost too horrible to consider, but in some weird way, if he was Mellisande's sire and she was Bobby's, and Bobby's was mine, then we *were* freakishly somehow related. The thought gave me the heebie jeebies, and I wasn't sure what it meant, if anything, in the vamp world. When all this was over, if we lived through it, I was going to search Melli's place for some kind of handbook. I was tired of feeling that everyone else knew the score but me, that there was some kind of play going on and no one had given me my lines. I didn't even know the plot, or when the trap doors might open up under me.

Just about everyone had beaten me to the dorm. Cassandra was passing out glasses of blood like a flight attendant. There looked to be barely enough in each one to keep us focused.

If we didn't die tonight, I was going to have to come up with a plan for keeping us fed. I'd probably have to do other fun stuff too, like find a way to pay electric bills. I could only hope smelly Melli owned her place outright.

I couldn't even believe I was worrying about all this stuff. *This* was why I'd never run for student council or anything else. Too much pressure, not enough reward. It wasn't like the head vamp got to walk the red carpet in Vera Wang, dripping in jewels with the paparazzi snapping pictures at every angle, but I guess that was the big diff between me and the dragon lady. I wanted the power to turn heads; she wanted to turn the minds in them.

Bobby came in with the last of the kids and put that supportive hand on my shoulder. "It's time."

I looked around the room, at all those fresh faces—some nicely framed with wispy bangs, others, like Marcy, in desperate need of a makeover—and my mouth went dry. As if she *knew,* Cassandra handed me the last little cup of blood, and I smiled gratefully while hoisting it up.

"To us and freedom!" I managed not to dribble any of it down my chin when I drank. They were a great audience. Those who had not already drunk raised their glasses and downed them with me. I had the spotlight; now I just had to figure out how to use it to best advantage.

"They're coming," I said simply, raising my voice enough to carry and bounce back at me threefold. No one asked how I knew. "If we let them in, there's going to be hell to pay. Anyone who survives the punishment will end up answering to some bigger, badder vamp and will never be totally trusted. And I don't know about you, but I've had enough of their little reindeer games. I like having my own room."

Folks cheered.

"So I need you all to grab whatever you can. Trevor, you head Team Alpha. You've got the basement and back doors. Bobby, you've got Beta. Take the front door and the rooms with vulnerable windows. We can do this!"

People cheered again, but not quite as confidently.

Trevor skirted them to bump my shoulder. "*You're* in Alpha. Are you with us?"

I shook my head. "There's something else I have to do"—which sounded like a total cop-out. "I'm going to search the dragon lady's office for blueprints or something," I quickly explained. "Make sure there are no more hidden ways in, and see if there's another blood or weapons stash somewhere."

He nodded, and my shoulders, which I hadn't even realized were tense, dropped to a comfier position. I didn't have the faintest clue what I was doing. Right now, approval was the only guide I had.

"Alpha, to me," Trevor called.

"Beta, this way," Bobby seconded.

The room split like the Red Sea. I took a second just to watch this group, which had totally become my new family. A warm and fuzzy feeling reared its ticklish head; my throat kinda closed up and my stomach clenched. This had to work. My classmates, every single one of them, had to live, or else I was going all Gina on someone's ass.

I slipped out of the room before I could go all gooey emotional and took the stairs two at a time to Melli's office. I started with the desk drawers, just 'cause they were easy. The top one wasn't even locked. It wasn't very helpful, either—paper clips, lipstick and eyeliner, miscellaneous bills, rubber bands, a dried-up glue stick. Totally useless—except maybe the makeup, which I swiped.

The other drawers needed more encouragement to open, and I'd just succeeded when a burly boy burst into the room, scaring me half to death.

"Bobby sent me," he said when I stupidly clutched my heart like an old-time heroine. "I'm supposed to watch the windows...and your back."

Fear made me snarky—like I needed an excuse. "My back's not about to do anything interesting, so you just focus on those windows."

On cue, the middle one shattered. I might have screamed. Burly—I was going to have to start learning names—whirled, his stake raised even though Bobby's punji sticks, or whatever he called them, were already on target—the body that came bursting through impaled itself. I braced myself for the horror, the writhing and shrieking, but there was none. The council—Melli—whoever, had launched an already-dead vamp through the window to trigger our defenses. I cringed at the thought, but didn't have long with it.

Above the body, where the glass had shattered but there was no stake to stop it, something came flying right at us. It hit the ground practically at my feet and exploded open.

I'd been looking right at it, and it hit me like a can of mace. If my lungs had been working they would have seized. My eyes teared up, blazing like an out-of-control forest fire. My nose dripped blood. A garlic bomb!

"Guy!" I called.

"Jim," he answered.

I held back my "whatever," because it *did* matter, and flailed blindly toward the voice.

"We've got to get out of here," I told him.

My hand caught one of his biceps and squeezed reflexively.

Together we stumbled toward the door. I bumped my legs on one of the guest chairs and blessed my vamp healing that it wouldn't even leave a mark.

As soon as we opened the door I could hear the chaos in the hall. They must have had enough garlic bombs to go around. I blinked about a thousand times per second, trying to clear my vision, but my head was swimming and between that and my eyes, everything was a blur. In the room we'd just left, it sounded like the window frame itself was splintering.

"Everyone, back to the windows," I called, my voice sounding like I'd gargled with razor blades. "They're coming through. Ignore the doors; they know we've got them covered."

Jim and I rushed back into the office, still blinking back blood tears. Thing One, all model gorgeous and feral as hell, had climbed over the cold, dead body of his compatriot to plant himself in the room. He'd teamed up with some chick I didn't recognize—had to be council—but it didn't matter. They were going down. My family wouldn't fall.

"Got an extra weapon?" I asked Jim out of the corner of my mouth.

Only he didn't get the chance to respond before they were on us. Thing One lunged for me, stake flashing directly for my heart. He used no finesse at all, like he didn't expect any worthy opposition. Defenseless, I shrieked, which would have been totally useful if I'd been a banshee or something, and leapt for one of the chairs, hoping to use it like a lion tamer against a feral feline. The legs were kind of like four really dull, metal-tipped stakes.

We danced like that, him faking right and going left, but I had enough coverage with the chair to fend him off. It couldn't last forever, though. I was no good to anyone in the thick of the fight while I was just holding my guy at bay. Then he surprised me with a stop, drop, and roll maneuver, which brought him in under my chair so he could slash at my ankles. I jumped back, smack up against Jim's back as he went head to head with the council lady— although "lady" was probably giving her too much credit.

But Jim wasn't used to this kind of fighting any more than I was, and when the lady lunged and he dodged, I was the one who got hit right in the shoulder by her pointy stick. My whole arm went numb, and one side of the chair I was holding dropped to the ground. Thing One took advantage and rushed in, and I had to drop the other half of the chair to block him. I swept my working hand up and deflected the stake just enough to make it miss my heart, though it pierced a boob.

"If they come out of this uneven, I'll boil your brains," I threatened, my teeth clenched against the pain. I'm sure I was *very* scary.

He snarled and tried to pull back the stake, but it was trapped between two of my ribs. I howled as he twisted and threw myself to the side, stake and all. With a huge effort, I pulled it out myself, spurting him with a burst of blood. My knees almost buckled, but I had a weapon now if not the strength to use it.

Thing One pulled another stake out of thin air and lunged for me again. My only chance was to outrun him, but that meant turning my back. From the corner of my eye, I saw the council conspirator go down, and I faked a swipe at Thing One to distract him while Jim stabbed him from behind. It seemed a crappy thing to do, but love, war and all that... I couldn't worry too much when it was kill or be killed.

"Thanks!" I yelled, running—more like jogging with my tanks on empty—for the door. "Hallway," I explained shortly, saving my strength. "See who else needs help."

We got to the office door just as the whole house started to shake.

23

The hallway was in chaos. It was as if the vamps had broken in on all sides, surrounding us. A bunch of the kids had retreated into the hallway and were in one big huddle, about to be mobbed.

"Hey!" I yelled at the vamps closing in. "Looking for me?"

It was a toss-up which was bigger, my ego or my mouth, but it had the desired effect. Those closest to me whirled, bringing me face-to-fugly-face with the dragon lady.

Her lips were peeled back from her teeth, which had

grown into a Hollywood cliché. Still, I wanted the name of her dentist, because they were blindingly white.

"Finally," she hissed.

She lunged—no warning at all, no witty banter. A showdown with my arch nemesis should at least involve a good monologue with plenty of time for a brilliant escape, but all I had was a split second before her hands were wrapped around my neck like a vice, her talons drawing blood where they dug deeply into my flesh. Since I didn't need to breathe, I wondered if I'd driven her beyond all reason or if she intended to cut my head off in teeny tiny increments.

I remembered the stake I'd pulled from my own body and managed to jab it into her hip, her chest being pressed too closely up against mine in a creepy, jigsaw puzzle kind of way.

She howled and leapt back, but I kept hold of the stake, which slid from her body with a wet, suctiony sound I'd carry with me forever.

"You bitch," she spat.

"Takes one to know one," I fired back. Okay, so I had to work on my one-liners, but I was under just a little bit of pressure right then.

She leapt for me again, this time batting my stake aside as I tried to go for her chest. My hand went numb at her solid blow, just like before. My only weapon fell to the ground and rolled straight under my feet. I went down, but I took Melli-noma with me—a combination of the momentum from her swing and the sharp crack of my foot on her shin as I fell.

She landed on top of me, and I kicked for all I was worth to reverse that, but she didn't play nice and in fact sunk her teeth into my neck as if she would tear it out. I forced my hands up between us, but they were slow and weak, and the light around us flickered ... or maybe that was my vision.

The strobing glimpses I got were not good. Jim going down with a stake to the chest, courtesy of Thing Two; Bobby with a club coming at his head even as he flung a hand out to disarm two council vamps with his power; Pam and Vanessa taking down unnamed blond chick with their water guns ... okay, that last one was heartening.

I tried to cry out a warning to Bobby, but then the whole place shuddered. A lamp crashed to the ground, shattering glittering shards over the floor, and a magazine rack thudded from the pile of junk stacked up in front of the door.

"Police!" called a voice with totally its own reverb. It sounded like he was on a megaphone and totally meant business. "Open up!"

Melli and I looked at each other, and for half a second we were totally on the same *oh crap* wavelength—only I'd bet the words she used were a helluva lot less ladylike.

"I *will* kill you," she snarled.

"You can try," I answered.

She pushed up off me. "To me!" she called to the others.

The invading vamps, those who could rise, looked at Mellisande. "I know a back way," she said. I silently wished her luck getting to it and moving all the piled beds in time to escape, but I wasn't up to pursuing them.

The door quaked again and the voice rumbled, "I'll say it again—OPEN UP!" The caps on the last two words were as clear as a cloudless night.

I looked at Bobby, Trevor, everyone who met my gaze. My heart all warm and fuzzy at the sight of them. And I had a sudden thought. While my crashing-graduation plan had been all about recapturing my life, I had all I really wanted right here. And I had an idea how to hold onto it.

"We could run," I told them, my voice carrying. "Anyone who wants to, I won't blame you, but I have an idea about how we can do this on our own terms. You just have to trust me."

"No." It was the voice of Tina-the-tramp, who stepped forward right up into my grill. I'd somehow missed her in my warm and fuzzy sweep of the room. "So far, your orders have brought the council and the police down on us. I say we put it to a vote."

I was so not in the mood for her petty party. Something heavy slammed into the door, knocking more furniture to the floor, and I saw the chance to take control rapidly running out. "Fine," I said, surprising her. "All in favor of Tina as our spokesperson, raise your hand."

I waited for hers to go up, as I knew it would. It left her open, and I popped her one right in the nose. She'd been a pain in my butt for longer than I could remember. It was about time for me to return the favor. And it felt *good*. Her nose crunched under my fist. I knew it would heal, but for now the satisfaction was enough. She howled and buckled to the floor. Chaz stared at me, stunned, eyeing me like he might be next, but I had way more important fish to fry.

I finger-fluffed my hair, straightened my war-torn clothes, and went to let the lions into the gate.

"We're opening up," I called through the door as loudly as I could. "We're unarmed."

I pulled off the first layer of junk and let it tumble to the floor. "A little help here?"

The others dropped their weapons and came to haul down the barricade.

"What's the plan?" Trevor asked.

"We're coming out of the closet."

"You're *gay?*" Tina asked, only it came out more like "Or *ay?*" and I totally ignored her.

"Someone called this in," I explained. "Which means it's probably been picked up on police scanners and everything. Even if Bobby could whammy everyone, there'd be no way to hide all these bodies indefinitely. The only other option is to run. If we do that, we'd have no safe haven— the council doesn't want us on the loose. We'd be hunted. But if we can make national news . . . "

He stopped what he was doing. "You're kidding, right? Think about the hysteria, the government, the testing—"

"Paranoid much?" I asked, even though I'd had the same worries myself. But I had a solution ... maybe. "All that requires secrecy. We're going to blow this whole thing wide open."

He gave me that look I was starting to own, the one that said I was totally crazy but we were just going to roll with it, and it got him moving again.

"I hope you know what you're doing."

"Me too," I muttered.

The cop's patience lasted maybe a half-minute more before he yelled, "What's going on in there?" The sound of moving furniture must have disturbed him. Interior decorators probably gave him fits.

"We were attacked. We put up a barricade to protect ourselves," I yelled back. "Give us a second."

There was silence outside, but I chose to take that as a good sign.

"Quickly," I said.

All we had left was a sofa and a gaggle of books that had been pulled from their shelves. It took only the promised second to move them.

I signaled for Katie to open the door and greet the police. She'd be the most likely to put them at ease—unless we were faced with Dumb and Dumber, they had to have found the bodies hanging out our windows, but there was no way to face Katie's prima ballerina looks and think "psycho killer." With any luck, they'd even have noted that the window glass had shattered inward and the bodies had to have been flung against us (or died attacking, if the police's time-of-death skills were anything like my algebra).

Katie gave me a betrayed look, but I'd smooth it out later. Meanwhile, at least she opened the door before any more pounding could take place.

Two cops stood there, to either side of the doorway as if we might have blasted them had they stood dead center. And they had back up. In a town the size of Mozulla, that was easily half the force.

"Officers," she said, her voice gone suddenly all breathy. "Thank God you've come!"

They looked really confused. Faced with a group of innocent-looking teens covered in blood, I guess I would have been too... until they saw Bobby, at which point their eyes hardened and the guns that had slowly begun to lower came suddenly back to center of mass... his.

"Hands up, boy," said the taller of the two in front. He had a gap between his front teeth, which was supposed to mean sensitivity or sensuality or something, but his rock-steady aim said otherwise.

I'd momentarily forgotten all about Bobby's *wanted* status. Now we were going to pay.

"There's been a mistake," I said, and the officer, who'd passed over little 'ole me in his visual scan before, went stiff with shock.

"But you—you—And he—"

His partner let out a whistle. "Ben, she's not the only one."

Ben looked, *really looked* at the rest of us and eased one hand off the gun to give himself the sign of the cross. "Sweet Jesus," he muttered.

A news van pulled up outside, just visible over the shoulders of Ben and (for lack of a better name) Jerry and their backup.

The door panel said News Channel 9, which meant either Chad Erickson or Sandra Barnes. I didn't even know which to hope for. Chad had the killer cleft chin, but Sandra and I could do some serious retail damage. She had wicked taste.

"Won't you come in?" I asked the cops, stepping up beside Katie to play hostess.

They looked at us; they looked at each other. Clearly kids thought dead and bodyknapped suddenly walking around and offering hospitality had stripped their mental gears.

"Sh-shouldn't we wait for the detectives … and CSI?"

"Please," Bobby said. "Come in."

It was said politely enough, but I could feel the power behind it. My body hair stood on end until my arms looked like the top of Marcy's head.

"You too," he added when Sandra Barnes raced up in her red power suit and matching stilettos. The way she worked those things, she could probably do a 20k run in them without even blistering. She'd even left her cameraman several paces in the dust, but both were close enough to feel the power of Bobby's invitation.

They all stepped inside, their faces almost slack, and as they passed me to follow Bobby into the dragon lady's den, I hung back to issue one more order.

"Refortify the back way, but aside from that, leave everything as it is. Even with Bobby's mojo, this is going to take some heavy duty convincing. It's best if we don't seem to hide anything. Oh, and let us know when the crime scene folks and all arrive, just in case they need a quick whammy."

Katie grabbed my arm, and her hands were cold, even for a vamp. "You sure we're doing the right thing?" she asked.

"I sure don't have any other ideas. You?"

She shook her head, and I squeezed her hands.

"It'll be fine. You'll see."

I straightened my shoulders, ran a finger over my teeth, and prepared for my close-up. I only hoped the camera caught us as mirrors didn't. If not, I'd be making my screen debut as the invisible woman.

24

The media circus had only started with News Channel 9. By the time we were finished, three major networks had sent crews, and while they clearly thought we were nuts at first, they didn't stop the cameras ... not until we were done anyway.

And that's when Sandra's cameraman did a quick rewind to review the tape. He startled, his posture going ramrod straight and eyes about bugging out. Based on his reaction, a second cameraman quickly checked his tape while the first guy looked back and forth between us and the camera, as if that would solve the mystery.

"Vamps don't show up in mirrors, or, I'm guessing on film," I explained, hiding my disappointment. "Do you believe us now?"

Sandra stopped staring at us and circled behind the cameraman to see what he was seeing. I couldn't help but notice it also conveniently put the cameraman between us and her, like a human shield. I took it back—she and I could never be shopping buddies. Now that I looked closely, those cool suits were nothing but really good knock-offs anyway, probably made in a sleazy sweatshop.

The first officer on the scene, megaphone man, said, "We're going to need the commissioner."

"At least," muttered his partner.

"I've got to call this in," megaphone cop said, to us this time, like he was asking permission.

Bobby gave him the royal nod, which almost gave me the giggles, but I wasn't so giddy as to give in to them. What had seemed so clear when I ordered the barricade to come down was now all fuzzy. Would they let us stay together? After all, this technically wasn't our place, unless there were any spoils-of-war laws on the books. Would they send us to our homes? Take us in for questioning? Would someone discover my misadventures at the mall? Was Trevor right in his paranoia that we'd be grabbed for some secret purpose, like creating the army's own super soldiers? And for which government?

Bobby reached over and gave my hand a squeeze. "I won't let it happen."

I narrowed my eyes at him, glad for a focus. "Are you reading my mind?"

"No, your body language. When you're worried, your brows get a little crease right about..." He put a finger to my forehead, right between my brows. "Here." I gave a little squeak.

Everyone in the room looked at me.

"Wrinkles!" I explained.

They all went back to what they were doing, totally unsympathetic.

"Eternal youth, remember," Bobby whispered. "It means never having to say you're wrinkly."

"Oh, thank God," I whispered back. When no lightning bolt appeared to strike me down, I relaxed. If we *were* damned, we couldn't be very high on God's *To Smite* list. And for the moment, no one else was after us. Which brought me to another thought: it seemed to me like the skin-care industry should want us every bit as much as the government. I mean, everyone in the world was searching for the fountain of youth and we'd stumbled right onto it. We could make a fortune just selling skin samples. Or build an empire creating our own miracle cream.

"Let's get shots of the rest of the house," Sandra said, already bored and lulled into a sense of security even in the face of all the weirdness she'd seen so far. I only hoped the rest of the world adjusted so quickly.

"Crime scene!" megaphone man suddenly seemed to recall, and loudly at that. "You shouldn't even be in here." To his partner he added, "We'd better establish a perimeter before the commish arrives."

"We'll see you out," I told Sandra, who didn't look any too happy about it.

"We've got that," megaphone cop said. "You two just stay put for the moment."

I was half tempted to salute but was afraid of which finger I'd use. So I just nodded demurely, although it cost me.

At least once everyone was herded out, Bobby and I finally had a second of alone time.

"Guess everything's changed," I said, proving my mastery of the obvious. I thought back to the prophecy. *Change* and *chaos*. Yup, we'd certainly accomplished both.

Bobby took hold of my chin, lifted my face to his, and I drowned in those depthless blue eyes. "The world is constantly changing," he said. "The best we can do is guide our own trajectory."

It was such a Bobby thing to say that I smiled, weirdly feeling that all was right with the world, whatever tonight's fallout was.

"Bobby, I l—" ooh, so close, "like you. No matter what, we've got it covered, right?"

As eternal declarations go it was pretty weak, but he seemed to understand, at least if the bone-liquifying, soul-searing kiss he gave me was any indication. I was ready to up and lock the door, if my legs would support me, so Bobby could continue that thought, but then an impossibly deep voice said from the doorway, "Is this a private party, or can anyone join in?"

We jumped away from each other like guilty teenagers. Which I guess we were, except for the "guilty" part.

Right there in the doorway was a man in a phat black suit—like midnight black, the best tailoring I'd ever seen. If he was armed, he kept his piece hidden and one hand casually in his right hip pocket. And, oh yeah, he wore his sunglasses at night.

"Holy crap," Bobby said in hushed reverence. "The Men in Black. They really do exist."

The man shut the door behind him, and I saw my dreams of freedom, fame, and fortune crash and burn. If some secret agent man really had come calling, he likely wasn't here to offer us a life of leisure and luxury.

He stared each of us down for a moment, and it was freakish not to see myself reflected in his shades. I wondered if I'd ever get used to it.

"Here's how it's going to go," he said, without preamble or even introduction. His voice was totally uninflected, like he was a prerecording. "My people are outside cleaning up the scene, sweeping it all under the rug. Your people are now our people."

Great, I'd gained and lost an entourage all in one day. It had to be some kind of record.

"What do you mean, *our* people?" I placed my hands on my hips. "Who are you?"

"I promise you'll find out soon enough. For now, you're coming with us."

"The hell we are," Bobby said, looking poised to spring some new attack.

"I'm afraid I'm not asking."

Bobby gathered himself like he was ready to fight for his freedom. I could feel the power gathering. Then the mystery man took his hand out of his pocket and let something fall to the end of its chain. Smelly Melli's medallion gone supernova, burning like a white-hot sun. It suddenly occurred to me to wonder whether the watchers Rick had warned me about really *had* been the council. Or at least, whether they'd all been the council.

"You see, we know," he said ominously. "Others will learn about your powers. We can't let you fall into the wrong hands. You can work for your country or you can kiss your life … and your girl … good-bye. That's all the choice you have."

Bobby and I looked at each other. We'd crawled out of the dragon lady's frying pan only to get burned up in the fire.

But, as always, my mind seemed determined to make lemonade. I put a hand on Bobby's arm to keep him from doing anything foolish.

"Let me ask you one thing, Agent X. Does this gig come with a clothing allowance?"

The End.

Acknowledgments

There are so many people I want to thank that I don't know where to start, so here they are in no particular order. I want to thank my wonderful agent, Kristin Nelson, for everything; Andrew Karre, the editor who first believed, for his insightful editing; and my new editors, Brian Farrey and Sandy Sullivan, for doing so right by my book.

I want to thank the Cross-Genre Abuse Group for abuse (of course) and encouragement; my husband and son, who will give me grief for not coming first, although they do, of course; my mother, who has always been my cheerleader; my father for photography expertise; my sister and the rest of my family for being weird and wacky in wonderful ways; the Red Hat Ladies of Wilderness Lake, who bought my first pseudonymous novel and are so fantabulous; Beth Dunne for loving Bobby and Gina and for contagious enthusiasm. I'd also like to give a shout out to the folks at the Igloo Café in Astoria, NY, which is a place of good writing, and the Tae Kwon Do studio in Queens where I did so many of my revisions while my son did his forms.

©Olan Mills

Lucienne Diver is a literary agent by day, a writer by night. (Hey, it's still dark at 5:00 AM.) Her credits include short stories and a romantic comedy written under the pseudonym Kit Daniels. With her young adult novel *Vamped*, Lucienne's taking off the mask and stepping into the full glare of... indirect sunlight. 'Cause as her heroine would tell you, anything else is hazardous to your health, especially once you've been Vamped.